PRAISE FOR CARLOS LABBÉ

"Begins to fuck with your head from its very first word."
—Toby Litt

"Labbé wreaks havoc on narrative rules from the start and keeps doing it."
—*Bookforum*

"Labbé deliberately distorts conventional narrative forms to create a
challenging but engaging text."
—*New York Journal of Books*

THE
MURMURATION

BY CARLOS LABBÉ

Translated by Will Vanderhyden

OPEN LETTER
LITERARY TRANSLATIONS FROM THE UNIVERSITY OF ROCHESTER

Originally published in Spanish as *La parvá* by Sangria Publishers, 2015
Copyright © Carlos Labbé, 2015
Translation copyright © Will Vanderhyden, 2024

Library of Congress Cataloging-in-Publication data: Available.
ISBN (pb): 978-1-960385-01-7 | ISBN (ebook): 978-1-960385-06-2

This project is supported in part by an award from the New York State Council on the Arts with the support of the governor of New York and the New York State Legislature

Cover design by Anna Jordan
Printed on acid-free paper in the United States of America
Open Letter is the University of Rochester's nonprofit, literary translation press.
Morey Hall 313, Box 270451, Rochester, NY 14627
www.openletterbooks.org

THE
MURMURATION

1
CLASSES

THE DIRECTOR WILL take the hand the attendant offers to help her up the stairs; she doesn't use it for support, though it may appear she does. Her arm rises or, rather, falls as she climbs the stairs, on her way to the first-class car. She releases the attendant's hand long enough to slip off one glove, which stops, hangs in the air, and continues on, clutched in her other hand, because the hand wearing it has left the rail to take hold of the handle that opens the door. The director thanks the next attendant and tells him to take the luggage to her compartment, her voice at once grave, sharp, intense, quiet; she listens with satisfaction as her words take effect, their resonance eliminating all else in the ears of the attendant who replies:

"At your service."

The director opens the curtain in her compartment's sleeper car ever so slightly. The light enters, casting her in shadow such that someone watching from outside wouldn't be able to see her: she's not there opening the curtain, she can't see anything out the window, though the platform is moving relative to her and the curtain and the glass. She doesn't touch the lamps, sit on the sofa, or use the ashtrays, and yet the lamps shine, the sofa is soft and inviting, and the ashtrays smolder for someone, whoever it is, who may be sleeping in that compartment, under her name, behind the Do Not Disturb sign that hangs from the doorknob all night. She closes the door, stays inside, or leaves and walks to the dining car, her footsteps not causing the floor in the hallway to creak even once: nobody sees her, sees them; nobody recognizes her, everybody imagines that she must have a male companion who will be coming in after her. The only person not paying attention is the commentator, absorbed in his steaming cup of matico, yet he's the only one to greet her with any perceptible gesture, inclining his head and instinctively lifting the hat from the seat beside him. An irregularity in the rails forces the director to drop into a seat at the adjacent table, and she sits there for the next hour; from the vantage point of the man in the corner, dozing behind a weekly paper, she boarded at the Temuco station and went directly into the dining car, and the cigarette in that glittering hand—her painted nails aren't visible to him—will smolder all the way to Chillán even though it's been stubbed out. The commentator sets his cup on the coaster, rummages in his pocket, there's a metallic scraping sound and the lighter flame flickers to life: they're not husband and wife, the waiter with a napkin over his arm realizes as he moves down the aisle past them; he was sure they were a couple who'd been together for decades when he saw them come in through the same door at the same station, and yet, not so; they're strangers, meeting now for the first time, he realizes this immediately when he sees the man offer her a light, and he puts away the handkerchief he just ran across his neck, crosses his arms in the doorway to the car, and prepares to guess what'll happen next: now the man will ask for the drink menu. But no, the commentator's eyes remain fixed on the infinity of interwoven trees outside the opposite window, he doesn't smile at the director, she doesn't smile at him either, and yet both acknowledge the other's gesture: she inhales, but doesn't let the flame touch the tip of her cigarette; he lowers the warm lighter to the table, and she, out of habit, breathes out through a space between her teeth, though she doesn't exhale smoke, and yet two, six, a whole pack's worth of cigarettes burn down to nothing between her fingers.

"A glass of Araucano, please."

The director raises her hand and her voice toward the waiter, the only person there who understands what she says as an order: the table is already set with silverware, napkin, liquor, and the contents of the bowl, every word that she utters and he writes down will eventually end up in a wicker trashcan in the kitchen car.

"Neat," she adds. "And some olives."

In the end, even the serenity of the director turning the pages of what she is and isn't reading—a book and also a magazine, pure propaganda—stands out against the calm of the commentator as he shifts his gaze from one tree to the next, looking out the window into the fading twilight, under the rain, as his forehead tilts toward this or that hill, and as his shoulders absorb the jolts from an irregularity in the metal of the tracks and the train enters a clearing that suddenly opens up out the window, speeds past adobe houses, dogs, children who come out of the mud and start running, expressions of urgency on their faces, after the express train, until the wood of the bridge bursts violently into view and the valley opens up and with a clatter, the rumble that never stops returns; for the blink of an eye it seemed that all the men in the dining car were equal in their deafness, all of them dressed in suits that looked shabby alongside the cream or violet or red of the director's dress or, maybe, her lack of dress in the imaginations of some of those men who don't look at her yet can't stop looking at her in the dining car: she sat there all through dinner and is still sitting there reading, she hasn't left her compartment, yet everyone knows she boarded the first-class car, and when the waiter—he's been watching her without watching her too—brings her drink, the polished shoe on her foot, firmly placed, invisible at the end of her long leg, gets in his way and down he goes, the tray with napkins, glass, notepad, is sent flying and, with a crash, falls on the indifferent figure of the director, who doesn't shriek or cry out or complain, she doesn't even lift her hands to her drenched torso, her voice just releases a brief string of words that—like the bonfire burning between four houses they just passed, like the lantern at a rural train station and the person wearily holding it up even though the express train doesn't stop for the eyes of the commentator, still looking out the window—everyone immediately forgets, her voice (they won't even remember that a woman had been in the dining car on the night the commentator traveled to the opening ceremony of the 1962 World Cup in Santiago) saying:

"It's fine, don't worry. Please. Just bring me a double cortado. No sugar."

Night has fallen over the passing landscape, just a solitary point of light, shining high in the distance, perhaps the glimmer of snow on a volcano or a cluster of stars or a slice of moon rising over the cordillera, or maybe another lantern at another remote train station; the director closes what she's been reading and it's possible she's just been flipping through that volume's pages, which no longer appear to be soaked with Araucano liquor, under the dining car's central light, glinting off the black thread of the curtains of the commentator's window which he's kept open, when the flash of a silver cigarette case in her hand attracts his attention.

"Would you like one?"

The commentator moves his head up and down and stays there, motionless, but she's neither looking at him nor at her own image in the glass (the waiter already came through to close the curtains of the second to last window), nor at the stained pages that her fingers and their red, black, purple—or, how scandalous, unpolished—nails have stopped turning. She reads the cover for the umpteenth and first time with his eyes: *Quién es quién, Deportivo mundial 62 / World Football Who's Who '62.*

"Care to have a look?" the director says. "Otherwise I'll send it with the boy to the trashcan. It's soaked."

No one but the commentator can hear her, and because her voice is so faint he doesn't smile.

"Thank you."

The director appears to lift the book with her fingers, though she's leaning back in her seat and smoking, who knows if she looks him in the eye. She doesn't smile either.

"You're very welcome."

For the commentator, she may be looking down and her eyes may try to meet his as she's about to open her mouth with a pleased sound, but the central light in the dining car is too faint to tell with the rain beating down on the roof of the southern express train.

"Even the best waiters trip and fall sometimes."

She must have let out a little laugh; but the sound is lost in the incessant thrumming, and adds:

"Let all waiters trip and fall at the same time."

The commentator turns in his seat. The director has indeed been sitting at the table adjacent to his in the dining car all throughout the eve of the World Cup's opening ceremony.

"Let all waiters trip and fall at the same time, but better not to let all of them drop their trays on me."

The commentator is finally able to see her and the movement—which she's trying to conceal—of slightly pursing her lips, widening her eyes, broadening her cheekbones, says to him that yes, that he has to look at her now, at that hour of the night when the few passengers who hadn't withdrawn to nod off in their second-class seats had gotten drunk, and the first-class compartments are too difficult to calmly return to, through the hallways illuminated by yellowish light. The director knows who he is, knows that he's the commentator, the sportscaster, there's no way she doesn't.

"To tell the truth, I don't really like to read with all this wobbling."

"Honestly, you don't have to read this dreck. It's just names. Long lists of names and numbers no one cares about."

Three tables away, two men are playing brisque, shirtsleeves rolled up and four empty glasses in front of them. Their speech grows more aggressive, making clear they're watching the two silent passengers. While to eyes of the waiter smoking between cars, of another passenger struggling with the crossword in the evening paper, of the four businessmen competing for control of the conversation amid Cuban cigars and aguardiente, and of the old drunk who's no longer drinking but has passed out on his plate, the director has moved down the aisle without a word; and yet there she is, a solitary woman, distant, attempting to convince that bored-looking man to do something; anything they can't obsessively observe is so outside the realm of possibility that their conversations drift away, mimicking the movement of a memory that animates the rhythm of the long night on the train, its clattering thrum echoing the voices of the women who speak to them in homes they're returning to or coming from, different yet the same, a vivid evocation conjured by the metallic screeching of wheel on rail, of the rusty door to the dining car swinging open as the waiter reenters, shivering, by the bell from a table in the back that's remained vacant all night, by a forgettable little shriek those women won't make, an assured response they can't translate:

"And I don't say that because I'm not interested in fútbol. I like it, but not because of the fact that there are twenty-two men pretending to chase around a piece of leather. Look."

The director gets up and sits down at the commentator's table. Nobody notices, nobody sees how her movement leaves no room for interpretation; everyone watches her. She stays there. Her handbag and her sliver cigarette case stay on her table, so they forget the woman: her movements are different from their own, she's traveling alone, and it occurs to them that there must be women like her everywhere. The eyes of the few men who are still sober no longer seek out the director, maybe because she's not alone anymore, in the dining car, aboard the express train from Temuco to Santiago, with the curtains drawn, under the rain.

"Nothing but titles, positions, rules, salaries. The physical activity of the individuals herein is minimal. The game is totally watered down in these pages. You're a fan."

"Naturally."

"Look. Just three team pictures, not one shot of the players in action on the pitch."

"The ball doesn't make a single appearance either."

"Yes. I know they sent you one too."

The eyes of the director and the commentator don't meet questioningly; before they can, they're erased by the eyes of the men watching them, men who don't see them control their expressions, avoid uttering names and surnames and even nicknames, what they see are their professions on the table next to the ashtray, the teacup, the glass, and the tumbler; above all, they see their hands, which haven't stayed under the table yet aren't gesticulating in full view either.

"Let me tell you something," the director continues. "The players have the advantage of being able to strike with all their pent-up rage a possibility that comes at them high speed. Or to pass the responsibility off to a teammate. But neither you nor I can respond to an offer with a mere kick. They reject that round flash that comes at them, calibrating the hate they'll express in the shot and delivering it. That's why so many people—the poor proles as much as the tie-wearing bureaucrats and even the boozehound dandies in charge of organizing the World Cup—are interested in the game. Even if they've never set foot on a field."

The commentator's arm, already obscured at that hour, moves across the surface of the table as his interlocutor speaks, he's the only one listening to her, because by now he's realized that she's there to tell him something specific, even if, as an attendant walking through the car imagines, she never left her first-class compartment. It seemed like the commentator was wiping the surface of the table when he answered her, after draining the last sip from his teacup.

"Anyone would think you play soccer."

The rapid movement of the director's four fingers indicate that at any moment she'll get up and return to her compartment, and the few men not watching her imagine her moving down the aisle in the direction of the first-class bathrooms, which nobody would be watching over at that hour, because they're spacious, have running water, and, above all, mirrors. The movement of her four fingers is precise: she takes the dish with olive pits, the already-empty shot glass, the napkin holder, the metal lighter, the half-wrinkled pack, the stinking ashtray, and arranges them.

"Anyone would think you played soccer when you were little."

"They never let us. Never, except among ourselves. Before I became a woman, I even tied my hair up in a bun, put on a wool hat, struck the ball and raced across the field, I slammed my soles into the shins of the fastest boy and absorbed kicks in front of the goal without complaint. But in the end, the boy who owned the ball always came over to talk to me in a low voice, giving me a wink and saying why don't you bring some bottles of Bilz next time, or asking me to help him make a new ball, a better one with rags from my house, or to take one of his socks that needed darning home to my mom, or to touch the injury on his foot. They smell us and get inhibited, so they form clubs and rage in other ways when they lose. They learn how to behave when there's a little girl in the game, they see themselves from outside through her eyes, and want to be the boy who controls the ball during the game and to become the sensitive boy when the game is over. Even when they're grown up, sitting around, putting together commissions, boards, committees, and divisions, they only accept a woman at the table because they want to see themselves on the front page of the newspaper where, because of their position, they'll never get to be, and so for them the mere gaze of someone who doesn't play the game turns what they see into a photograph."

Each of the director's fingers reveals a nail the color of the darkness in the car, there's only the reflection of the central light—dwindling in intensity—off the glass objects. Tables beyond, the drunks guess at the cards the man facing them is hiding but can't decide at a glance whether her fingernails are painted or not, whether it's the right or left hand, or—this seems most important to them—what her other hand is doing, whether it's above or below the table.

"Your colleagues won't admit it," she continues, "but at every meeting of gentlemen, the man speaking wants to be heard as if he were on the radio and someone else were narrating what he was doing."

The commentator avoids looking at her. He lowers his eyes and finds that the dish, the shot glass, the napkin holder, the teacup, the lighter, the cigarette pack, and the ashtray are laid out in four lines. Now they're objects, shapes, homogeneous pieces asking an inaudible question in her voice, coming and going with the sway of the train. Then he interrupts her:

"Is that why you decided to become a director?"

Her fingernails are painted black, that's the only possibility in the night. One of her hands is under the table and for the man—who, three tables to the left, leaning on the curtain, is nodding off but isn't asleep as he makes his observation—it passes across something invisible. Her other hand removes one of the pieces from the table, the goalkeeper.

"Right. To take ownership of the ball. But that was a childish idea, an errant notion that got me into the cult, into the club, got me a seat at the conference room table. The truth is that the ball has one owner and the stadium has another. Those owners agree to elevate certain players—to bring them up from the dirt field—who produce profits for the ball and the stadium. Radio, and in a few years television, has other owners who form a partnership with the owners of the ball and the stadium to expand the reach of the whole enterprise, until it is everywhere, until it fills the eyes and ears of people who themselves, when they were little, chased after that rag ball in the dust. The eyes and ears of all those people become the property of the same individuals who'll never let a woman enter that space, unless she's half-naked and holding up a sign."

"So then you already understand why I've refused to work in television."

The director removes another three pieces from the table, a fourth, and then two more when the waiter comes over with his tray, disrupting that opaque exchange of glances, presuming the woman has something to say to him. The commentator puts his hand on the last piece, the one that belongs to her. The director removes it.

"This is the center forward," continues the commentator. "He scores the goals and is incapable of speaking to the press, he adorns the front pages of newspapers and the covers of magazines, he's a brute, but garners the attention of the owners. The boys and girls on that dirt field you mentioned shout his name and nickname whenever they score a goal. But none of it works if this center forward is out there all alone. These days they want to turn the game into a soloist activity, with close-up shots and reporters who hang praise on the figure of the superstar every time he touches the ball."

"Precisely."

"They want, based on what you're saying, to make as if there are one or two team owners on the field as well, to obviate the possibility of horizontal organization, the importance of the community, the mere idea of which can at times be a threat to them."

"That's why I became director."

"They want to erase the English word 'team' and replace it with the far more generic Spanish word 'equipo.' Addicts and fans will be turned into followers and spectators who at first will assume the plural implicit in the definition of 'equipo' that refers to the whole, to the team, but soon they'll get used to the fact that 'equipo' also refers to 'equipment,' to tools, to individual parts of a machine. Now, with this World Cup, they're trying to eliminate the team, just as they're doing with the syndicates, the fishing collectives, the agricultural cooperatives, the small-scale mining organizations, the workers' groups, the literary movements, the student unions. Now, the profile of the player, the star, is all that'll matter; they'll even elevate the individual figure of the reporter above the communications team, and, at the same time, they'll offer him a column in some unimportant newspaper so they can keep him around for fifty years and when he dies they'll honor him as the founding father of Chilean journalism; they might even put his name on the Campo de Sports stadium. Other reporters will overrun the space occupied today by poets and writers, but only one of them will be the chosen one, the protagonist, one and only one in history: one liberator, one hero, one capital city, and one country."

"That's why I became director."

"And that's why I retired from sportscasting."

The train shakes as it goes down a hill, crosses a bridge, enters a forest, and emerges into a small town, where none of the residents refer to it as the express train but use other names impossible for the language of this nocturnal conversation.

"That's precisely what I wanted to talk to you about."

As the rails shake again, the only figure left on the table falls to the floor, rolls down the aisle and, no longer an ashtray, glass, lighter, or teacup, reaches the space that separates the dining car from the car behind it, and, for an instant, hangs in the air like a useless—nameless—object before shattering against the rocky ground of the railway.

"I'm listening."

The director opens her mouth and the sound of crystalline rain falling on the roof of the car swells into existence, rain that ceases almost instantly as she conceals her laugh. The rain stops and the commentator looks at her, surprised by her unexpected reaction, because he can't see that, behind him, the four businessmen have gotten to their feet and are leaving the game of brisque behind and approaching, bumping into tables, passing by, one hand on their hats, the second touching their belching lips, the third on their waistbands, and the fourth clutching billfolds so full they barely close; they're struggling so hard just to stay on their feet that, in that moment, all they see is the narrow aisle, the single bed in their compartments, the coming darkness, maybe a chamomile tea upon waking to forget what's happened here and to settle their stomachs, at which point the commentator and director, the only shadows still moving in the dining car, will have disappeared from the Santiago railway station.

The waiter isn't seeing them anymore either. All he can see are the three or so possible hours of sleep he'll get on the warm floor of the kitchen car.

"You can stay here as long as you like, but we're stopping service."

"That'll be all. Thank you." The director takes a moment to react, reaching out her hand to the man in an instinctive gesture where what's striking aren't the pale bills in her outstretched fingers but her fingernails, which, to the waiter, are definitely painted purple.

"At your service."

The waiter understands. He bows his head, doesn't bother to straighten up the last table—the table where the drunk had passed out, before being escorted by two men to a seat in second class, because he was unable to pronounce his name or last name or number or profession—and walks out, closing the doors to the dining car behind him.

"I'm going to be direct. How much, or what, would it take to get you to return to sportscasting? They need you for our team's performance in the tournament and I need you too. Those are two different things, but there's only one answer. We've talked with the radio people; they're prepared to move things around so that tomorrow you'll be in the booth to call Chile versus Switzerland. It'll be six matches total; the pay is generous. You can even rest your voice during the third match—if you suffer from the aphonia, which, I've been led to believe, can be caused by the dust at the Campo de Sports during the winter—once our team has already qualified. We'll let you know ahead of time, but I can tell you now that certain individuals are of the mind that Chile must lose that third match against Germany."

"Wait. You assume rather quickly that I'm not surprised by your offer."

"The thing is, it's not an offer. It's something far less courteous."

The director is sitting up straight now. She doesn't have to keep still anymore, her frame and legs and waist and neckline and shoulders and hair and face and hands fully materialize at the table now, in front of the commentator, because there's no one else there to see and immediately erase her, so she gets to her feet, leans over the table, and draws back the curtain. She doesn't care that the commentator can see her full form from behind, out the window rises the imposing cordillera of the Andes, shooting up between the clouds, beating a retreat now, transparent against the dark, soon to dissipate, leaving the night fully illuminated by the moon.

"I'm not here on behalf of the Federation. I have a mandate from the Ministry, signed by the president himself."

The commentator focuses on the glass, looking at the director's back, the curtains between her fingernails, which have begun to grow out, leaving behind small unpolished spaces at the base. They still have no answers.

"Look at that," he says.

"That horse!"

"It's not a horse. Think about how far away it is. It looks like a horse because of its shape, but it's not.

"It's a gold horse. I can't believe it. White, yes. It's going so fast."

"Exactly. No horse runs that fast. Look closely."

The director is convinced. She's not looking out the window, but at the body in front of her.

"It's a swarm of Solstice fireflies. I haven't seen anything like that in a long time," he adds. "And now it'll become a whirling burning bush."

The color change of the phenomenon they're witnessing is subtle, the director knows that no transformation in itself is monumental—whatever it is that's following them through those pastures at such speed is not—but is always precarious. Only in that way, gradually, does it ever assume an apparently definitive form.

"And now they'll come closer."

The luminous mass, another color now, suddenly swells, it's the perspective that makes the myriad insects expand, slowed by the weight of a small light, dancing outside the window and dynamically converging into a lush, vertical shape—one of hundreds, streaking across the incessant landscape of the clear night outside the express train—illuminated as the commentator says:

"And now they'll make a tree."

As his voice rises in intensity to add that the Solstice fireflies are finally dispersing, in a blink the sky appears blanketed in stars—but no, the moon is out and the fireflies have alighted on the window, then the commentator presses his middle finger against his thumb and snaps, the insects scatter, and the landscape reverts to a succession of shrubs, large estates, shanties, barbed-wire fences, reservoirs, landfills, carriages. The director rubs her sleepless eyes. She sighs.

"I realize," she concedes, sitting back down, a furrow fading from her brow, "with this ability of yours, you could've devoted yourself to partisan politics. Your public speeches would've been incendiary or narcotizing, you could've inspired massive popular uprisings or broken up protests on the spot."

"You're mistaken. I can't say anything about movements to which I have only the most distant connection. What I do, my work, is not magic. Where I come from, people do it every day, and I know there are corners in other provinces, in other Indo-American countries, in Africa, even in less populated areas to the north, in deserts and on beaches in Asia, and on some plains of Oceania, where it's normal for the mere act of speech to become part of the surrounding choreography. A Cuban businessman told me once that the North American marketing laboratories are already successfully instituting a plan to control the movement of millions and millions of people through vocalization. For them, the key is the rhythm of the speech, and so they're selling radios and televisions with amplification systems where the main thing is the deep sounds; popular music, the Cuban called it. Look at what's starting to happen with the twist and rock 'n' roll in the dance halls in downtown Santiago."

"It's all part of a greater project."

Her nails, now pearlescent in the faint glow of the flickering light, rummage aimlessly inside the pack of cigarettes, her movements slow because her counterpart's eyes appear fixed on the symmetry between her urgency and the incessant landscape, shadow after shadow, leaf after leaf, tree after tree, branch after branch, stick after stick, twigs, splinters, papers, fire, smoke. They are the only two passengers in the dining car at this late hour: her gesture sweeps away some absence and allows her to take the offered lighter so she can light two cigarettes with her hand of glittering fingernails and pass one to him as she continues, smoke billowing between her words:

"A project so great that a bunch of local fat-cat directors will never be able to understand it. Not even the part of the organization chart that includes them."

The commentator turns to take a drag on his cigarette, listening. The main light in the car goes out as a poorly maintained rail converges with an irregular one, such that the silence adds to the darkness and stops them from even wanting to wonder if the interruption was due to a defect—in which case, in a matter of seconds the racing between cars, the flashlights, the voices calling for calm, and the screeches would begin—or, rather, to a switch being intentionally flipped in the engine so that anyone still in the dining car would feel discombobulated and return to the place where the fatigue, the sleepiness, the lack of curiosity of the railway owners deemed it appropriate for everyone to take refuge at that hour.

"Is that to say that it's a project without structure, that it won't unfold in space, but over time?"

"Exactly. You said it: time. That thing that the local enemies and the foreign backers of our government, both together and separately, call History; progress unleashed until it reaches the inflection point."

"And you, who work for both, need my voice, my narration, at the World Cup of Soccer to precipitate it."

"Please, don't get me wrong."

The director inhales the smoke deeply, and as she does a new side of her face is illuminated for the first time through the cloak of darkness that's fallen over the train. Her eyes and his remain fixed on the reflection of those different features in the window, then it's only her eyes, astonished because a moth is fluttering outside the glass, seeking the incandescent tip of her cigarette; and yet, the train advances at a speed impossible for the flight of any nocturnal insect.

"Listen, please."

A blink of complacency from the commentator precedes the moth breaking apart into a multitude of minuscule insects that, as they come to a stop, are whipped away by the wind and lost from sight.

"Forgive me," he says.

"I don't need your narration for the whole World Cup, just for the Chilean team."

Lacking an ashtray, in the darkness the two of them have begun to form a heap of ash in the middle of the table and, though they can't see it, they know that if either of them raises their voice, sighs, or snorts, they'll get ash all over the other.

"It's not enough that the middle class is finally coming to grips with what it is to go into debt, to apply for credit to gain access to record players and televisions; it's not enough that our working masses are comprised of semi-autonomous individuals who sing and dance, the awareness produced in them by the twist and rock 'n' roll won't suffice. Irrational consumerism and erotic subjugation only take place when there's a larger, more powerful, arbitrary, competitive, and impassioned collective framework.

"Has the impact of the wars with Peru and Bolivia worn off then?"

The mountain of ash in the middle of the table collapses.

"It was important. Of course. But the foreign backers of our government no longer tolerate half-measures in the business of war. They want monopolies. They'll propose that we unite with our trans-Andean colleagues, but at the same time they'll direct the Argentinians to partner with the Brazilians, perhaps to split up Uruguay. Ever since they went off the rails, national wars in Central Europe of the last century are no longer commercially viable. Besides, who wants the British and the Yankees to take over all the small towns again without being required to pay any tax or a single tariff."

The clattering of the train softens, and with its constant sound, its lack of rhythm, their dialogue is lulled into slumber for a moment, allowing them to glimpse the corporeal forms of the night, sitting still and staring out at the moon or at a mass of water, a river, a reservoir, a canal, a puddle left by the rain in the blink of an eye.

"It's clear that you know whom I've voted for over the past twenty-four years. You know where I come from and that nobody wants to say my second surname. You know how they mocked me in the Normal School, which is why I left. You've heard the way I pronounce the *ch*, the *tr*, the *u*, the *ng*. Why would I want to devote myself to making the Chileans an even more arrogant, blind, and deaf race?"

"Because, just like me, you know well that there's no such thing as race, much less a Chilean race, one Chile, and some Chileans. Because what I am asking you to do is to use your narration to bring them to the brink of collective ecstasy, to the edge of national climax, to the point of the full and mass blossoming of a proud, fervent, indefinable, worker-driven, class-proof identity. With your narration, the Chilean team will bring the idea that there exists something like Chile to the imminence that our trans-Andean siblings achieved nearly a decade ago, to that state the Prussians attained with their idea of Germany. And when those fans have finally glimpsed the brink, the edge, instead of showing them how to keep climbing, you'll push them over it, so they fall. We need to lose just when we're about to win, so the certainty that our fulfillment was within reach and we let it go remains as if imprinted on our people. We don't want this country to turn into Brazil, Mexico, or China."

"I see."

Out the train window, the silhouette of the hills has begun to draw itself in blue. The director's hands collect the tobacco ash, mound it up, shape it into small lines that, from above, admit the possibility of a scaled architectonic form: a labyrinth, a stadium, a bunker, an island, the interior of the Casa de Moneda, circumvolutions of the cerebrum, a dense plot of streets that, when their design is complete, will begin to be called highway; on her fingers the nail polish seems to have paled like the dawn.

"And what makes you think that such a thing won't just be another seed, something that sooner or later will explode into unrelenting violence against the palaces of Santiago?"

"I knew we would understand each other," says the director. And her hands reach out over the ash, unexpectedly open. Her face is finally illuminated for the commentator—whose own face still reflects nothing and doesn't smile—who, hearing her, is once again the narrator.

"A few years ago," she continues, "I was working at Ferrobádminton's club headquarters, at Estación Central. One day, on my way home, walking to the bus stop, through the same catcalls, threats, whispers, and groping as always, I turned down one of those side streets between pedestrian walkways, one that no longer has a name because it's been changed so many times. It was the middle of winter, like now; it was dark, but not cold, there was a boxing match and the bars were full of drunk men listening to the radio. I avoided a group of students, turned down an alley, and there, for the first time, I saw a person whose name I won't mention: she was smoking outside a tenement door, eyes open but unseeing. Younger than I, she was the most beautiful person I'd ever seen. The impression was so striking that I couldn't stop and continued on my way to catch the bus. From that day onward, I took that roundabout route every day, hoping to see her again. For five years, every afternoon and every morning, with no luck. Until on a day like any other, I gave up; tired and confused, I took a different route; when I sat down in the trolley, feeling so sad, someone sat down beside me and spoke in a strange voice. The voice startled me: it was her. What a surprise to find you here! she said. I thought you lived near

Estación Central. I always see you pass through the neighborhood, she continued. I looked at her. I wanted to touch her face, to tell her that I'd been looking for her all this time, to for a moment stop caring what everyone else thought, but instead I shrugged, raised my eyebrows, and got off at the next stop. I never saw her again. And do you know why I didn't say anything to her?"

"Please, tell me."

"Because despite the fact that I'm a director, I'm still a woman, not a man. Because my name is already being erased from the proceedings of this World Cup. Because, even if I'd dared touch her, I would never have been able to do what I wanted to do with her in public, something thrilling: something any man, even a complete deadbeat, can do anytime and anywhere without a problem, in any open area in any town, or along any lost highway in the middle of nowhere, without anyone being surprised or scandalized."

The bang of the dining car's rusted door interrupts the conversation. A uniformed attendant, shaven, fresh, says good morning, announces that they will be arriving at their destination in forty-five minutes, and asks if he should have the waiter bring them breakfast or if they would prefer to return to their compartments to rest.

2

MURMURATIONS

HERE IN THE Estadio Nacional, on the Campos de Sports, we'll be a people of eighty thousand: just so, faithful listener, cheering on our team's combinations. With silence we'll set our screams against the accumulations and variations of the other team. We'll turn this World Cup semifinal into an endless succession of kicks and missteps, into howls and ovations, into the silence of eighty thousand of us running alongside our twenty-two-man team down below, alongside the twenty-five players out on the pitch, and hopefully, for a while, we'll warm our bodies, exposed to this winter wind, the same wind of so many winters past.

We'll start waving our handkerchiefs. Photographers will flutter around the formations, expectant listener, our team in red and white saluting the humming crowd, a timid booing for the still-crossed arms and the faces of the eleven Brazilians, still smiling for the firing squad of flashes, seeking to capture the official photograph. In the stands, we'll care more about the distribution of red shirts and blue socks; the white of our team's shorts, all one across the pitch, will orient the angle of our handkerchiefs and seat cushions at the foot of the mountains that crown this Wednesday afternoon—the thirteenth day of June, in the year 1962 of the Christian era—with snow. But there above, attentive listener, there will still be empty seats in your luxury box.

The match will begin with the evolutions of the Brazilian team, the defending world champions. Forwards Vavá and Garrincha, dear listener, will await the whistle of Liman referee, Yamasaki Maldonado. Receiving the kickoff from Garrincha, Vavá will touch the ball back to him, the rest of the team already arrayed in position. Zito will send a pass to Zagallo, who will lose it to our defender, Raúl Sanchez. With Sanchez we'll see Eladio Rojas downfield and try to get him the ball, but Didí will intercept it and look to move it back to Zagallo, breaking to his left. But his pass is weak and we'll cut it out with Pluto Contreras and take control of the ball with enough time and space to slow down and look around: we'll make a run down the right touchline—to your left, listener—with Eyzaguirre knowing that Raúl Sánchez will be trailing him, providing support in case of an error or pressure from our opponents, and that, at the same time, in the middle, a few strides ahead, we'll have Jorge Toro who might be a better option, even though Zagallo will probably be all over him, and also that, across the pitch, beyond the black blur of the referee, we'll be moving more diffusely with our left defender, the guerrillero Manuel Rodríguez, and our left wing, Leonel Sánchez. And yet, with Pluto we'll pass the ball to Jorge Toro and send it along with him to our other wing, Jaime Ramírez Banda, who'll touch it back to a breaking Jorge Toro, with whom we'll catch it in stride and deliver it quickly to Eladio around midfield; the uneven surface will prevent our midfielder from settling the ball for a quick pass, so we'll pull up and let the play develop, waiting for our teammates to make runs, to drop back in support, to make eye contact, to find a passing lane, but the canarinho shirts will outnumber our red ones in that part of the pitch and we'll be indecisive; they'll move symmetrically to apply pressure, forcing a rushed pass of predictable trajectory toward our forward, Honorino Landa, that will be quickly intercepted by the opposing defender, Mauro Ramos, who, knowing Didí is open, will one-touch the ball to him, and Didí, in turn, will send a searching ball in the direction of Zito that'll sail unexpectedly long and land in front of Zagallo, who'll corral it quickly and deliver it without hesitation to Vavá in the center.

Your luxury box will remain empty, dear listener. We'll close in on Vavá with Pluto and Jorge Toro to make a play on the ball, but he'll hold his own and fend us off; Vavá will maintain possession and continue downfield, but the ball will get away from him, and we'll step up with our right defender, Eyzaguirre, to collect it and scan our team's formation across the pitch, all of us taking a deep breath, trying to find our initial position in the shape that we've just begun to delineate on the field. But the referee, Yamasaki Maldonado, will think that seconds before he saw us clearly make an excessively aggressive tackle on Vavá with Pluto, so he'll blow the play dead to punish our infraction with a free kick. Their other forward, Amarildo, will bend down to position the ball, but surprisingly it'll be Didí who'll run up behind him to take the kick; but the ball will go out over the goal and we'll watch as it sails harmlessly through the air, far away. And far away you'll still be, listen to me.

We'll place the ball at the edge of our goal area with our keeper, Escuti, and then send it along with Raúl Sánchez to Eyzaguirre with whom we'll quickly touch it on to Jorge Toro and then err with him when we decide to carry the ball toward midfield, searching for a passing angle, because Vavá will catch us off guard, sliding in and striking the ball fiercely but imprecisely toward our goal, but the referee, Yamasaki Maldonado, will stop play and call a foul on Vavá for his tackle on Jorge Toro, prompting some forced applause from us for the fucking *chesumadre* referee, despite the somnolence of the Ñuñoa afternoon. And out of the corner of our eye we'll also see that a valet in a white jacket has emerged into the luxury box from an interior gallery, a brilliant white tablecloth folded under his arm and a box of equally resplendent napkins in his hands, and will right away begin to set a small table behind the plush leather seats, not caring at all that a free kick has been called in our favor.

Raúl Sánchez will strike the ball from the middle of our half of the pitch toward the players we'll have making runs into the center circle. But the ball will drop closer to the canarinho players and their defender Zózimo will leap up and head the ball to a waiting Nilton Santos along the right touchline where, under pressure from Honorino and our wing, Ramírez Banda, he'll drop it back to Zito, who will switch places with Zózimo and send the ball out to Nilton Santos, who will deliver it quickly to Zózimo in the middle and get a one-touch pass right back from him. We realize that they're shifting into a shape that we've discussed at length: it'll resemble a zigzag, but that's just the opening move. We'll have our own shape too. And theirs will continue to develop with the left wingback sending a searching ball toward his canarinho teammates in the attacking end, a long pass that won't reach their forward, Garrincha, because we'll cut it off with Raúl Sánchez, controlling the ball with a firm header and continuing across the pitch, altering the rhythm of the moment, some of us will stand up in the bleachers because, holy shit, we'll be dribbling the ball with the feet of Honorino and closing in on the opposing area when Mauro Ramos will come sliding in and collide with Honorino in unison with Yamasaki Maldonado's whistle; a good call by the biased referee, the unjust, bribed *saquero*, who walks over, left hand raised, booking the infraction and awarding us a free kick. Listen, this is true: we'll have risen in silent protest, arms slack and fists clenched at the opposing player, at the valet setting the last of the silverware on the buffet table be-hind the plush seats in that luxury box where you won't yet have appeared. Just listen: as our opponents form a wall, we'll spread out strategically, awaiting the kick from our right wing, Leonel, who, arms akimbo, fifteen meters behind the ball, will observe us, ready himself, and take a breath; we'll hear the whistle and run with him, all eyes on the ground now because we'll want to hit it hard, and then Leonel will decide—him not us—to strike the ball with his right instep, so it won't clear the leaping wall of Brazilian defend-ers. Better to sit back down, fucking hell, forgive us; the valet will set the last silver knife on the table, but the ball will continue on its path toward their goal, slowly, and we might have controlled it with our center forward, Armando Tobar, if not for the fact that Mauro Ramos will step in first and send the clearance so high that it'll come down on our side of the pitch, where only two of our defenders have stayed back to cover a canarinho forward who runs and runs. But we'll stop their attack with Raúl Sánchez and cheer in the stands when, seeing our wing, Ramírez Banda, along the right touchline, we send him a quick and direct pass and—listen—that's how we'll have to initiate our corresponding shape: a lateral opening. We'll carry the ball with our wing, Ramírez Banda, and then drop it back to Eyzaguirre, slightly behind, continuing our run with our wing, so we can send it back to him. We, in red, *La Roja*, are realizing now that, if nothing else, our shape could exist; the same thing will gleam for a second in the eyes of the valet, standing stiffly, another spotless napkin draped over his shoulder: he's waiting for you, attentive listener, we know you're coming, but not with whom, not how many, not why you're in their company, you who will have asked to listen to this broadcast on the radio of the vehicle in which you're riding, the vehicle that's approaching the stadium now.

Instead of going to Honorino in the center of the attack, we'll pass the ball back to our right wing, Ramírez Banda, even though he's covered by Zito and Nilton Santos. Because we'll be looking for a different way to get the ball to Honorino, sending a looping cross from the right corner into the center of the canarinho area, but the ball will sail long, past Honorino's position, and land at the feet of Djalma Santos, back in our opponent's possession, in the stillness of the valet and two of his coworkers, there above in the empty luxury box, in an external flow that'll begin with the other team's feet and arrive at ours without us yet understanding how to construct a collective movement. We'll only have to pay attention to our keeper Escuti, to our passivity, to the ball that, distant, will come and go between us with neither precision nor commitment, because you'll only be hearing this, because you won't be paying attention to us, because the luxury vehicle you're riding in won't yet have parked.

We'll recover the ball with the feet of our defender, Raúl San-chez, a red spot on our waving white handkerchiefs, and deliver it to Eyzaguirre on our left, touching it on with him to our wing, Ramírez Banda, and then dropping a deft ball back to Eyzaguirre so we can slash downfield with Ramírez Banda; we turn back, opening up to receive the pass. The luxury vehicle you're riding in will have come to a stop. Will you still hear this broadcast when valets appear to open your door, to offer you a hand of false sup-port, and you set foot on the sidewalk? With Eyzaguirre, we'll send a long ball back in the direction of our wing, Ramírez Banda, and yet, along the right touchline the opposing defender, Nilton San-tos, will dart in and disrupt our combination with a header. His teammate, Zózimo, will possess the ball, protect it from us, and deliver it to Zito on his left. We run. We jog. We walk. Zózimo will hesitate, the ball at his feet, waiting for his teammates to make runs, to find open passing lanes; he'll carry the ball through mid-field, coming right at us, moving into our penalty area, and when we rush at him like a waterfall, he'll send a pass to his forward, Amarildo, whom we'll pursue with the guerrillero Rodríguez, and listen: we'll throw up our arms, motherfucking *conchelalora*, because the ball will bounce off our opponent's bicep as he goes to the ground to trap it and the volume of our protest swells, for fuck's sake, *por la chucha*, with the confusion and the blown call by the referee, *hijo de su hijo*, nevertheless Amarildo will find a way to get the ball to their right wing, Garrincha, even though there are four of us in the area, four of our players who will unintentionally mimic their zigzag because we just saw them do it, and you're still nowhere to be seen. Garrincha will recognize the play immediately and swing the ball away from our pressure with the guerrillero Rodríguez back out to Amarildo, who will turn and streak toward the far left corner, leaving us behind, finding the last feasible angle on the pitch, and sending a looping cross into our penalty area, hoping the ball will be tracked in the center by his teammate, Vavá, or maybe Zagallo, trying to slip out to our right as we push up into the ball's path, or even Zito or Didí, who will converge with us a little ways back to win the ball we'll think is ours, and in the end it's Zagallo in front of our goal preparing for the strike, but we'll step up with Eyzaguirre and cut off the ball's parabolic trajectory and start pushing up the pitch while you, you and the men accompanying you, walk wearily toward a private access point into the stadium, a dozen briefcases and one handbag: that's where the tips come from that the valets have been awaiting while surreptitiously glancing at the clock that doesn't seem to be ticking, and their ears will remain focused on our breathing, on the cheering of the name of our wing, Ramírez Banda, you'll hear our laughter in the stands even in the belly of the stadium, because we'll send him the ball with Eyzaguirre and begin running, clinging to that right touch-line, its chalk as bright as our handkerchiefs, waving so frantically we won't even see their red spots and, taking advantage of the fact that multiple canarinho players are slow getting back, we'll push up toward Nilton Santos, who will appear poised to pounce, so we'll pull up and cut toward the middle, slowing again like you and the men accompanying you in front of the security guard who will hold the door for you with excess deference. We'll be wanting to settle into a shape we've caught glimpses of in previous matches but not yet found out here under the cordillera of the Andes, in the cold, as the afternoon's languid, secretive quality slips away; everyone will be in place but you, and we'll pass the ball to Eladio in the center circle so we can sprint downfield with our wing, hoping for a long return pass, but with Eladio—and without you and the men who are just setting foot on the most exclusive stairway in the coliseum—we'll still be thinking about that more important shape and will try a different play: we'll pass it to our forward, Honorino, a few paces to the right, quickly steering it back to Jorge Toro and making a run toward the goal; we'll push it out to the right with Jorge Toro to Eyzaguirre who, stretching the field, will chip the ball down the chalk touchline to the waiting feet of our wing, Ramírez Banda, while, with Honorino, we'll slash parallel through the middle of the opposing line, and only then will you become fully visible, hearing this now through the loud-speaker in the vestibule where one of the men you're with will sit down to catch his breath because the stairs have left him tired and he's used to his staff carrying him everywhere; the opposition's staggered-triangle shape will have come into clear view, the same shape they'll have used to contain us and previously to fend off the masses; the staggered triangle whose base will be built of play-ers who defend by attacking, one of whom, Zózimo, will recognize the combination we're attempting with our wing and Honorino, and, anticipating the pass that'll open up a shot on goal, will step up and send the ball away with a hard clearance, so hard it'll go out across the chalk touchline and the game will come to a halt, unlike your footsteps, yours and those of the men accompanying you, ascending the final stairway to the luxury box, and you'll brush the hair from your face, attentive to my words; you won't be able to locate me among the fans, in the tribune or the stands, but in all the jaws clenching in frustration as, instead of being directed on frame, the ball will sail out across the touchline.

Standing with our wing, Ramírez Banda, on that same side of the pitch, we'll take the ball from the ball boy and make the throw, back to Pluto and send it with him hard up the pitch to Eyzaguirre. To the right, we'll press the attacking line forward with Honorino, our center forward, Tobar, and Leonel trailing to the left. We'll look to drop it back with Eyzaguirre but opt to cut across the top of the *canarinho* area, outpacing Zagallo and skimming the ball across the grass toward the waiting feet of Honorino, ready to strike it on frame, but their defender, Zózimo, a foreigner, an exquisite talent, will deflect it with the side of his foot and send it away from goal, hoping that, in support, the inscrutable Nilton Santos will have more options, running to our right and sending a pass to Zagallo as the rest of the team shifts into position, listen: what I'm saying is that their triangle will suddenly resemble a rhombus, our goal the blunt tip, and in that flash our shape will appear constricted, an hourglass, stretched thin, two clusters with nothing connecting them but a narrow passageway, that's how we'll see and cease to see ourselves in the moment that Zagallo will already have passed the ball to Vavá, and Vavá on to Garrincha, and we'll know that you'll hesitate too, unsure if you should keep walking to the luxury box or excuse yourself to go to the powder room, to find the telephone and make the call, and taking too long to check the positions of Didí and Amarildo, Garrincha will turn the ball over to the feet of Leonel, shit let's go, *vamos miércale*, with whom we'll hesitate and elude Vavá before looking to pass, on the attack at last, in the stands cheering *chichichí*, *lelelé*, we'll hold off both Zózimo and Zito, you'll finally be taking in the entire stadium, the view opening out before you as your drove of directors arrives to the box of honor, five minutes into the game, your eyes on all of us, the roar from the crowd for the play out on the field that's about to break down, because, in the end, Zito will get the ball away from us but won't be able to corral it either; the ball will skitter across the grass and if we can't possess it with Jorge Toro they might be off to the races, Didí might appear out of nowhere, so we'll spring into action, lunging after the ball with Leonel, but the sturdy Zito will block our path, and as usual the rage will send us sliding into his legs, motherfucking *conchesumadre*, so you'll see us tackle him hard, striking his left foot, you who will be watching and listening, feeling everything we see and hear when the *saquero*, the slow, *desgraciado*, sellout referee will blow his whistle because we'll have fouled Zito with Leonel, there, down on the field; we'll scamper away from referee Yamasaki Maldonado, shouting, telling us to cool it, the council of international directors will have already arrived to the stadium, you'll be there—tell me your name—and through the insults we're drunkenly spewing, we'll show you our missing teeth, because after the whistle we'll go over with Leonel to offer the referee the ball, and when Yamasaki Maldonado, *chesumadre* motherfucker, gets ready to receive it, we'll mock him by tossing the it away from his executioner's hands to a canarinho player, and maybe then our laughter will be yours; that's how we'll want you, even with your face obscured by the hazy glass of whiskey the man next to you is holding, because you have yet to reveal your name.

Djalma Santos will place the ball at the edge of the center circle for the free kick. Our laughter will fade as they try to reestablish their shape. Knowing that Mauro Ramos is coming up behind him, Djalma Santos will jog off to the side so Ramos can touch him the ball while the rest of the team spreads the field, moving into their triangle shape. Now Djalma Santos will strike a hard ball, sending it high toward our side of the pitch, dropping it in the space Amarildo will have run into, just inside our penalty area, and even though we'll step up with Raúl Sánchez as if to clear him out of the way, he'll get a touch on the ball, directing it to Garrincha, who will confuse us coming down the touchline to our left, but we'll stay on him with the guerrillero Rodríguez and won't take our eyes off him, and you won't take yours off of us, off the speed of the players' legs coming at us, and before Garrincha is able to deliver the ball to his teammates who're trying to push into our area, in desperation we'll throw ourselves at the feet of the canarinho player with the guerrillero Rodríguez and all that we are, and the ball will skitter across the chalk touchline, but the thieving Peruvian referee, Yamasaki Maldonado, biased beyond belief, will almost step on us where we're sprawled on the grass in his rush to blow the whistle—piece of shit ref—and signal a corner for the Brazilian team.

We'll scramble as Garrincha places the ball in front of the left corner flag, as he blinks and surveys the—for us—indecipherable movement of his teammates, as they shift into the shape of a receptacle that, with just one pass, will transform into an inverted rectangle whose corners will push into the white lines of our penalty area, and we'll realize that among the suits and ties and shoes in the luxury box, among those gleaming bald spots, those impeccable haircuts, and those massaged backs, you'll be the only one to sit down and watch us, crossing one leg over the other, hidden amid the silver of the trays that another five valets dressed in white will keep bringing out throughout the match, and you'll hear how we fall silent as the skillful touch of Garrincha's corner will send the ball bouncing toward Amarildo, who will battle Raúl Sánchez and the guerrillero but won't be able to get a foot on it: they believe in their shape, but we'll hold firm on our field, knowing what's coming, and being closer, we'll make a play on the ball, with all our rage, and clear it away from the goal that you and the others there above had reinforced before this World Cup started. The ball will shoot high into the air and drop in a parabola at the feet of Leonel, but we'll fail to control it with him, relinquishing possession to Zito who, within a second, will see Garrincha stalking down our left side once again; Garrincha will receive the pass and we'll chase him down and strip it away with the guerrillero and Raúl Sánchez, the men behind and in front of you will keep us from seeing your face, the expression you make as you follow what we're saying: how, with the guerrillero Rodríguez, we'll possess the ball and move toward midfield, waiting for a space to open up, how Didí or some other opposing player will hound us until we deliver the ball to our wing, Ramírez Banda, and how, nevertheless, instead of continuing to run to the right—that place in this formation that will always seem so truly ours—we'll turn toward the middle again and drop the ball back to the guerrillero, with whom we'll want to wait for a teammate to make a run downfield but then will send it anyway, just in case, right as Djalma Santos reads the play and stretches out his left foot to intercept the ball's linear trajectory, but we'll recover it with the guerrillero and continue our run that we'll soon realize won't ever reach its destination, beyond what all of you up there in the luxury box are discussing, far from your eyes and ears here, rising and turning your back on us, because you have to greet a group of arriving diplomats, individuals and names you despise in equal measure without saying so, but their wing-back, Djalma Santos, will be running too, faster than us with the guerrillero Rodríguez, and he'll trap the ball with his right foot, the one that only appears more potent; he'll take possession and send the ball back, back into the canarinho area, where Mauro Ramos will strike it hard so that it rockets up and drops down on our side but far from our control, into the space where Zagallo will have stayed, Zagallo who will one-touch it a few feet back to Zózimo; with his teammates already spreading out across the pitch, tracing diagonal lines, Zózimo will send a driven ball to our left, an area of persistent trouble for us, and the ball will reach the feet of Vavá, who will have managed to sneak behind us. We'll want you to sigh along with us as Vavá makes a slashing run, faster than our Raúl Sánchez, now that you'll have retaken your seat in the luxury box, though all that we can see of you is the glass of sparkling water in your hand. We'll want you to sigh with relief because the Uruguayan linesman, Marino, will have raised his flag to indicate that the cana-rinho team's play has left Vavá in an offside position, an illegal position, theirs, and yours when the transparency of your glass will be lost behind the golden glass in the hands of a man with a double moustache who is approaching you. We'll set the ball down with Raúl Sánchez in the center of our half and put the free kick into play, sending it toward an analogous position on our oppo-nent's half. But the ball won't reach its intended target, the feet of our center forward, Tobar, because Didí will come out of nowhere and get there first, sending it forcefully back into his team's intangible attacking shape, toward the player always positioned along that touchline whom our left eye will repeatedly fail to see—Garrincha; your eyes will remain glued to the ball and your ears to these words. Garrincha will possess the ball and shift it from one foot to the other, stepping up against the guerrillero Rodríguez, with whom we'll an-

ticipate his next move and take the ball away and deliver it to Leonel, hoping with him to surprise them by sending the ball toward
the midfield line, and now yes: you'll move your dangling foot, one
leg crossed over the other, because you're hearing the beat of an
orchestra, because with a smile—invisible to us—you'll impel a
group of kids to leap across a river drawn in the dirt with a stick,
and imagining that, we'll construct a shape of two parallel lines
that advance in unison: we'll trap the ball with Jorge Toro, touch it
along to Eyzaguirre, and send it diagonally to our wing, Ramírez
Banda, all of us running in unison, without a care, without hesitation, without hurry. *La Roja* on the rise, trying to work our way
into the opponent's area, we'll drop the ball back to Eyzaguirre
with our wing, Ramírez Banda, and continue our run, split, simul-
taneous; you'll gesture to the man with the double moustache, trying to speak in your ear, to leave you alone and let you focus on
what we're doing down on the field, but with Eyzaguirre, instead of
continuing the combination, we'll split into three, incorporating
Jorge Toro and running with him toward midfield, looking for a
sign, your gesture, a glove waved in the face of the mustachioed
man who still won't leave you alone, and Jorge Toro's gesture to
Eladio Rojas. We'll turn on our axis with Eladio, waiting for the
guerrillero Rodríguez, along the opposite touchline, the one we
would've forgotten if it weren't to our left. We're about to send the
cross when Didí and Djalma Santos overtake us to cut off our run,
but before they can, we'll get the ball over to Tobar, and with Tobar
we'll once again change the rhythm of your foot, tapping on top of
your crossed leg, and then the man with the double moustache will
put a hand on your knee to stop you from standing to follow the
play, because if you did our wind would whip right through the
main balcony and we would see you, so we'll accelerate with our
center forward, Tobar, leaving Djalma Santos behind and as we

run you'll move with us; and from there, cutting in obliquely from the left, just outside the canarinho area, we'll finally take a shot at our opponent's goal. But the ball will sail high, away, passing close to the left post, and in the gallery, we'll scream, *¡casi conchetumadre!* almost, fucking hell!, even all of you there above will have leapt out of your plush leather seats just as you were feeling the urge to spill your glass of sparkling water, to splash the arthritic hands of the man with the double moustache. But no. Not yet. We're still goalless here in this World Cup semifinal between Chile and Brazil. And their number one, Gilmar, will take the goal kick. And it'll sail all the way across the field to none other than—you guessed it—Garrincha; now, with everyone sitting again, all of you there above having dropped back into your plush seats, your shape will be lost among the bustle of the valets who have returned carrying silver trays laden with canapés. Another member of the council of directors, a clean-shaven man lounging in his chair, will write a note on a piece of paper that he gives to the man beside him, and the paper will pass from hand to hand in your direction; better to let the ball's parabola drop at our feet, the feet of Raúl Sánchez, with whom we'll send it forcefully back toward one of our forwards just outside the canarinho box, but Vavá will cut off the ball's path, finding a way to jump in front of it just as it leaves our foot and the circuit will be altered, shifting now into their shape as the ball will deflect toward Nilton Santos, their right wingback, so oft our antagonist, who will head it on to his wing, Zagallo, closer to the border of our area, along the same right touchline; he'll turn away from our eyes, hiding the ball between his feet, and then retreat, looking for one of his teammates. We'll pressure him with Eyzaguirre, trying unsuccessfully to get the ball, and in the end the paper will reach the hand of the man with the double moustache, beside you, and he'll hold it with a smile, trying to catch your eye, just like us, though we'll know how to hold it when, instead of coming up with the ball, we step on the right cleat of Zagallo. Some of us will get to our feet in protest, because the referee, Yamasaki Maldonado, black suit, suspect, enemy collaborator, won't be seeing the entire picture: he won't see you either, so he'll penalize our tackle with a free kick. Nilton Santos will put the free kick into play, sending it toward midfield where Zózimo will be waiting, as their forwards and wings push up in a coordinated movement, then Zózimo will one-touch the ball into space for Garrincha, but he'll run too fast, too fast the smile of the man with the double moustache, wiped off his face by one your hands that we'll glimpse at last, leather-clad and gleaming, and too fast we'll have to be with the feet of Pluto Contreras to keep the ball from entering our red defensive area. The ball will keep bouncing toward our end of the pitch and Zagallo will collect it, two strides into his run and already picking out who in their panorama is prepared to take the shot and who in our box is wearing red. And how will Vavá come at us; you'll raise the question without asking it as you uncross your legs and smooth your coat with your black gloves, as you rebuff the man with the double moustache, who will have leaned into your ear, concealing the paper in his fist. Within the silence with which you do not answer him will hang the question of how Vavá, with his back turned, will be able to leap up, separating himself from the rest of us, and find the ball in a bicycle kick, holy shit, *un chilenita, por la cresta,* the cry that'll burst from the stands as the strike turns into a pass to Amarildo, whom we'll pursue with Pluto and Raúl Sánchez, and, eluding us, he'll drop it back to the top of our area, awash in red now, into the space Garrincha will come running into, and then your black glove will grip the hand of the man with the double moustache, and with your movement the open arms and bent body of Garrincha will slash through our defense and strike the ball with fury, but you're not holding the man's hand, you're squeezing his fist, and Garrincha will put a spin on the ball that we won't anticipate with our keeper and it'll rise as the man with the double moustache opens his mouth soundlessly and releases his clenched fist and the ball continues on its path to our right, ever our ruin, grab it motherfucker, *conchesumadre*, but it'll escape us, as your glove deftly snatches the paper from his fist, and bend back in the air toward the center of the frame so unexpectedly that we won't even comprehend the path of our own curses as we're left standing, helpless, fixed to the pitch as the ball sails inside the post for a goal. Goal. And you won't look at the paper. Goal. Goal for Brazil. They'll hug each other and we'll beat the bleachers with our newspapers, handkerchiefs, and seat cushions. We won't yet be capable of complaining, of turning on all of you there above with shouted threats, because the play will have shown us that, in a plural plot, Garrincha's shot, though virtuosic, will always be coherence and never individuality. The Brazilian team will have taken a one to zero lead over us, but in so doing they'll have shown us how to match them, how to find you: we must incorporate every move, even surprise strikes from the right, into what is ours, into the past and into the future out on these fields.

Attentive listener, you'll have ignored the celebratory embraces and complaints down below. Just as the canarinho shirts will gleam in the weak light of the June sun, and ours, red on white, will mesmerize, the paper will stand out against your glove, having been carefully folded to fit in your palm, yours being the only body that we catch a glimpse of from down here, shrouded. So we'll set up in the center circle with Honorino, drop a quick pass back to Jorge Toro, and run through midfield with him, eluding opponents, trying to alter the momentum of this game that's getting away from us, sending the ball on to Leonel, who will be open to our left, but we'll have rushed to put our plan into action and won't be able to contain the ball with Leonel and it'll go out into touch. Djalma Santos will hold the ball in his hands, taking his time, surveying his teammates and seeing Vavá make a run, and there's no way to stop our opponent's arms from extending and flexing, and likewise you'll have to wait to open your gloved hand until the valets return carrying trays laden with caviars, *cacerolas*, and brochettes, so the council members will forget about that slip of paper they passed over to you, to that place in the stadium nobody can clearly see, and Djalma Santos's throw will fly in a high parabola, almost to the middle of our red-spattered area. But we'll dart in with Raúl Sánchez and get in front of Vavá and cut off the throw, touching the ball to the guerrillero Rodríguez, always on the left, and continuing with him in an ascending scale, a shape only discovered with the other team's goal, revealing their fluid contrast to our winter stiffness, and to the glances the lounging members of the council of directors, already somewhat drunk, cast its way, your inviolable glove won't yet be a fist; an ascending scale through the center to Jorge Toro, turning to the right with him and sending the ball to our wingback, Eyzaguirre, whom we'll run with down the touchline across midfield, chased by Amarildo, and as we collide with Zagallo, the ball will bounce away from us. And yet, Amarildo won't be able to corral it either; but we'll stretch out Pluto's foot, deftly touching the ball in the direction of Jorge Toro, reestablishing our flow, and Jorge Toro's run will take us slashing between Zito and Didí as they step up to dispossess us, and your glovehands will remain but a blur; leaning as you'll now be against the railing of the luxury box, your back turned, your long coat taking on the color of the canopy but also showing through the white line of valets such that we'll catch a glimpse of the way you bring one

hand to your pocket. You'll have held that position, listening atten-
tively, because before Zito and Didí can catch Jorge Toro, we'll
touch the ball quickly to the right, to our wing, Ramírez Banda,
and with him we'll look up again and see a spot of red near the
indistinct darkness of the referee, and your left glove, hovering
briefly above the hand of the clean-shaven, red-faced man, the one
who, since the Brazilian goal, will have already amassed three
glasses of distinct size beside him. Then your left glove will return
to the railing: the red spot will resolve into one of our forwards
streaking across the withered mass of these winter grasses, surrounded by canarinho shirts, closing in. With our wing, Ramírez
Banda, we'll strike a hard ball with a high follow-through that'll be
intercepted by the leg of another, the leg of Nilton Santos, deflecting our parabola into one of his own, more concise; and yet, we'll
collect the ball with Eyzaguirre and settle into possession, just as
the dance of your left glove across the cheeky hand of the clean-
shaven man brings a smile to his lips; and we'll keep dribbling with
Eyzaguirre toward the right, away from the pressure of Didí, who
won't be as worn down as we are by all this booing and cheering,
so he'll appear faster and we'll be forced into making another im-
perfect pass, with no clear target, slow, lateral and backward, as
incomprehensible as the movement of your glove, if it weren't for
the fact that the clean-shaven, red-faced member of the council of
directors is smiling now, baring his front teeth and bringing a kerchief to his broad forehead to wipe away sweat, despite the cold
that can already be felt here, creeping into the gallery; he'll set his
glass on one of the valet's trays, glance at you with eyebrows raised,
and start walking over to one corner, to an area where we can just
make out silk-embroidered tablecloths atop long tables, the gleam
of three types of forks, four different knives, and two spoons at
each place setting, serving utensils for salad, seafood, and meats,

corkscrews, linen and paper napkins, tea sieves, individual coffee pots, toothpicks. But you won't go with the red-faced, clean-shaven man to the corner, it's not yet time for you to make your move or for us to make ours: we'll jog to retrieve the ball with Jorge Toro, his eyes our eyes, observing a shape that'll finally spread the length and width of the pitch, waiting for a run that'll tell him where to send the ball. But no run is coming, not yet, so we'll drop it off to Pluto, pushing up into a parallel position, in the middle, a few steps away, and with Pluto we'll turn to take on an approaching Zito. But no. Better to send the ball back to Jorge Toro, much better, and maybe with him we'll be able to find one of our shapes again: your shape for a second, gloved hands in pockets, because, unlike the clean-shaven man who wants you to follow him to the corner or the other men lounging in the luxury box, you'll feel the cold of this June afternoon too; we'll have opened up space on the pitch with Eladio and will receive a quick pass and try to get away as Didí and then Mauro Ramos come at us. They'll slide in and send us tripping and falling with Eladio. They'll get the ball, but not our screams, *conchesumadre* motherfuckers, away from us and turn and start immediately playing the ball down a vertical line of cana-rinho shirts through the center of the pitch, in the direction of Garrincha once again; we'll move in with the guerrillero to strike the ball without looking, without seeing you, as hard and as high as possible, only caring that the ball drops on the opponent's half of the pitch. And we'll run with Pluto to stop it from being sent right back, trapping it with our chest and bringing it down to our foot, looking to pass, but, shit, Amarildo will come sliding in from behind to kick it away from us. And we'll add the raised arms of Eladio to our shouts at the referee, as you'll finally remove that paper from your pocket with your right glove and referee Yama-saki Maldonado, his honor, will blow his whistle to stop the game because Amarildo's dirty tackle was a foul. Then we'll spread out across the grass, our white handkerchiefs moving the red shirts of our players into a triangle at the top of their area, facing off against their defending rectangle, listen: after multiple touches of the ball, paused in the center of the opponent's side of the pitch, we'll step back with Jorge Toro to run, to accelerate, to deliver a strike that instead of rising will stay on the ground, driven in a straight line, and yet, *carajo*, it won't penetrate the rival area because they'll go to the grass with Zózimo and send it bouncing back with his right foot in the face of our attack, in the face of our shouts, our cheers, our frontline rushing in behind our attacking forward, and one of your legs will once again cross over the other, now that you've sat back down and a valet has approached you for the umpteenth time to offer you a drink; in the face of our attack, Zito will stretch out his leg in a single movement that, nevertheless, won't block the path of our driven strike on the ball that, instead, we'll control with our wing, Ramírez Banda. We'll pass and run, all as one, in the direction of Eyzaguirre, but like every other time, we'll strike it too hard, too far, trying to do too much, and fail to get him the ball in front of their goal. It'll sail away from their goal and we'll never see what you're reading on that piece of paper or your expression as you react to it; all we'll see is how, without exaggeration or hesitation, you'll crumple it in your gloved left hand and drop it into a glass of water that'll depart on one of those golden trays.

Their keeper, Gilmar, won't wait even four seconds to pick up the ball and throw it out to his teammate, Nilton Santos. He won't wait, they cannot let us lie in wait for them just as we cannot let them lie in wait for us; and so, we'll come running to catch them off guard with Honorino and for once we'll easily trap them on our half, red over green, but that won't prevent their defender from dropping the ball back to his keeper, from solving the situation by running left. Then they'll pick up the ball with Gilmar's hands again and throw it to a breaking canarinho defender, who will send it hard toward midfield, moving quickly to confront us once again, red and white, your glove black which you might've brought to your face hearing this, not wanting anyone to notice that you too will have seen the man with the double moustache walking toward the corner, to your right, where workers and valets are still setting up the banquet for the council of directors; then you'll begin speaking in a low voice to the clean-shaven man, whose expression is an invitation; then Zagallo will be there, but when the ball drops it'll take an unexpected bounce back to us at midfield, where we'll control it with Jorge Toro and push up into the opposing half and prepare to attack along the horizon line of their penalty area. As we're deciding where and how to pass the ball, Garrincha will move in from our left again and take it away from us with such skill that we'll be left lying, befuddled, on the grass with Jorge Toro, and the ball will be sent to Amarildo, who will touch it on to the player with the best team vision, Zózimo. Jogging, Zózimo will quickly drop the ball back to the area of the pitch on our left, to Garrincha, who appears to limp, who is wily, who will make himself seem approachable, easy, playing dumb the bastard, the *desgraciado*, and almost get past us, past both Raúl Sánchez and Eladio, but at the last minute we'll realize that we need to get the ball and we will, sending it quickly along to Jorge Toro, with whom it'll always be better to move to the right, watching the guerrillero along the left, and sending it across to him, running deranged along the touchline; you'll read the paper in your black glove, not concealing it, motionless, and almost unable to see you, we won't know if you're ecstatic or livid, then we'll question the left side of the pitch and pull up with the guerrillero Rodríguez and pass it again to Eladio in the middle, slowing things down. Our block of reds shirts will all turn white, though now we'll be advancing into the half of the pitch where the opposition, the yellows, the greens, the canarinhos, fast, smiling, sly, will guard what's theirs as if they'll win just by moving. With each stride with Eladio we'll lose heart, pushing tentatively toward Zito, who will step up without hesitation, so better to drop it back a few feet to where Jorge Toro is supporting us, and with him we'll begin the circuit: Eyzaguirre to the right, ahead along that same touchline to our wing, Ramírez Banda, the ball at his feet; we'll have to pull it back, protect it under the sole of our cleat, and turn back, because we're being pestered by Nilton Santos, Zito, and Zagallo with little kicks and slaps that nobody will see, just as nobody will see your face, or your torso, draped in a coat the color of the winter afternoon, listen, and we'll find a way to send a pass to our center forward, Tobar, all of us running with him toward the corner, only Nilton Santos chasing us now, so they'll already know, the members of the council of directors there above will know—the men lounging around you, raising glasses of various sizes, laughing, but we won't see you laugh unless they want to force a response from you—who among us will be waiting for the pass, and with our center forward, Tobar, we'll try to find space, somewhere on the attacking end of the pitch to send the ball into with our whole body, without it being cleared by the defenders, and we won't find it because Zito will get his legs in the way and Nilton Santos will take the ball and send it across the right touchline, striking it with such force that we'll realize that they're learning something about us too, that not only will we be watching you, but that you'll be watching us too, that above all you'll be listening to us, waiting for the right moment to touch the council members in a way that'll make them fall to the floor, that one and another and all the directors will be left on the floor, and your face won't even be seen because your head won't be there, because absence of absence, because yours is the last figure in a massive succession of valets, chauffeurs, secretaries, assistants, butlers, co-ordinators, agents, and others who so far, so far, will have made it too easy for their orders to be carried out.

With the accelerated realization that we'll all learn something in trying to beat whoever is in front of us, we'll pick up the ball with our center forward, Tobar, and throw it in to Honorino, with whom we'll quickly lose it to Nilton Santos and Zito and watch in silence as it moves through the Brazilian area to the hands of the opposing keeper, Gilmar, fists clenched, except that now one of your gloved hands will reach out to grab a glass of sparkling water from another passing tray. The holiday feel of this June afternoon will transfer its rhythm to the game, we'll stop jumping to our feet, cheering, whistling, even turning to watch as their keeper, Gilmar, moves wearily to his left, rolling the ball from his hands to Nilton Santos, who will see that his collective hasn't yet assumed their assigned positions, so he'll send it back again to his keeper, away from us. Gilmar will run through the canarinho area bouncing the ball as yawns bounce around the luxury box, though none of them will be from you, if you're hearing me well, upright in your leather seat, holding your elbows to keep your shoulders open, shoulders that we'll have just glimpsed in the crowd of directors; their keeper, Gilmar, will bounce the ball again, while looking out at his teammates, just like your fellow council members and unlike our thousands of booing mouths, until their shape comes together, and then he'll strike the ball, sending it rising across their entire half of the pitch to fall on the far side of the center circle; we'll revel in the harsh music of our booing as your long leg, crossed over the other, moves to the rhythmic sounds our mouths are making, and out there in the middle of the pitch the ball will drop at Didí's feet. The fluidity of his touch, knowing Zagallo is running to his left, will interrupt our abrasive chant; we'll barely have time to blink because their wing, Zagallo, won't want us to catch him with a running Eyzaguirre. Zagallo will move the ball once, twice, three times from one foot to the other, cutting across the chalk line at the top of our red area, for a moment, eluding our defenders three, four times, letting the other canarinho forwards catch up; they'll wait for his pass in the center, but he'll flow toward the other side, toward Garrincha who, already surrounded by our red, our blue, our white, will come at the guerrillero Rodríguez at full speed and keep running until we shove him with the guerrillero, until, shit, our attention is drawn away from the ball, watching your movement up in the luxury box, pulling one leg slightly away from the other, maybe preparing to get to your feet, whereas Garrincha will fall to the ground in the middle of our box in unison with the whistle of referee Yamasaki Maldonado, *mala leche*, spiteful, never trust a convergence of arbiter and noise, the foul on Garrincha will have been obvious to you as we'll see, your movement to rise from your seat like the replica of a vague smile, a moan, an answer: the red-faced, clean-shaven man will have folded his hands, pleased that he's finally managed to draw you to his corner. The referee, Yamasaki Maldonado, surprisingly, won't punish our tackle with the maximum infraction of a penalty, but with a mere indirect free kick, just inside that area that all along will be our place, weakness, and origin. From shouts that we'll mistake for those of our keeper, Escuti, we'll converge three of our red and white shirts into a wall, fourteen steps from the goal, in front of a distant Garrincha, with Amarildo behind him, who will take the free kick quickly, not waiting for the whistle, forcing us to jump as the ball traverses the box and turning us all into animals of winter: when it goes wide right and over the endline, we won't utter a word, just a grunt, a rush of air escaping our noses and mouths, like that of the clean-shaven *desgraciado* and his drunk fellow-director with the double moustache, seeing you get to your feet, adjust your handbag, arrange your coat on the back of your seat, and walking over to them at last.

Then we'll hurry with the hands of our keeper, Escuti, we'll have to plan better from our goal. Along the ground across our whole area we'll pass it toward midfield, where now it'll be the moment for us to find a coherent shape: you, from your seat, moving directly toward the two council members who will have come together and separated in their directorial inebriation; we, with Jorge Toro, moving to the right, insistently, until with the faster wing, Ramírez Banda, we'll step up to receive the ball and deliver it to the middle, where we'll now be pushing up in a column; though crooked and irregular, a sweeping movement will be building, beginning with Leonel, whom we'll try to get the ball to on the left, but the way is blocked, so our pass won't move forward but parallel, lateral to Eladio, and we'll send it with him out to Jorge Toro on our treacherous left and start running with him, seeing that the column hasn't yet shifted into a triangle or sharpened point aimed at their penalty area, and picking up speed, not hesitating, moving quickly with soft touches on the ball, tracking your footsteps across the luxury box, over to the table where the two men await you. We'll send a driven ball to the left, but it'll stay too low to the ground and get blocked by a defender, along the border of the area belonging to the team they call Brazilians, canarinhos, *amarillos*; they'll intercept the ball and run it out of reach with Zito, sending a pass out to Nilton Santos on the right where we'll sense trouble, and where Santos will try to continue the circuit up ahead to Zagallo, but won't be able to because we'll bring pressure with our wing, Ramírez Banda, forcing the ball out across the touchline where we'll pick it up with Eyzaguirre and throw it quickly in to Jorge Toro, with whom we'll

be calling for it, but the arbitrary whistle of Yamasaki Maldonado
will intervene, demanding that the throw only happen once he's
given the go-ahead; you'll pause too as you calmly stroll over to
the table of devourers, directors, council members, enemies, your
back still turned as you remove something gleaming from the
pocket of the coat you'll have taken off at the insistence of yet another valet who will carry it to the coat check. Do you think that
running, jogging, walking, going to the ground and getting back
up one hundred times will be enough to overcome the cold of this
winter afternoon, in front of those drunken directors who will be
drawing lines with ringed fingers across the banquet tablecloth,
whose noses will try to snort up the powdery advantages of a vast
plan that'll turn the crowd of eighty thousand into millions when
transformed into a single individual, no longer a people or a crowd
of cheering fans, but one man who will fanatically carry out the
task he's given? And that object that you'll have taken out of your
pocket, that object that'll suddenly flash in our eyes, does it gleam?
We won't heed the reflection, in any case. We won't be dazzled; despite the cold, the sun will be shining down in our faces, so we'll
throw the ball in again from the sideline with Eyzaguirre, as the
flash of that object hits our eyes and we hear our own booing, and
we'll trap it again with the feet of Pluto Contreras and, again, shoot
it wide across the chalk endline: we'll still take pleasure in knowing
that your fellow council members, if they looked into that reflection, that flash, that gleam, will have realized that we care about
the integrity of the other team, about the rules, but not about the
ruling, the judgement, contrary to what they claim up there in the
luxury box, so many glasses in so many hands; we won't give a shit
that the referee, Yamasaki Maldonado, hasn't booked the kick we
delivered to the shin of Zagallo with our wing, Ramírez Banda.
We'll decide that you'll have briefly held a mirror up to your face,

pausing along your path from seats to banquet table, and although we won't see you in that reflection, you'll see us. Along the touchline, their forward, Amarildo, will pick up the ball for another throw and, as we're looking at the ground to conceal how we were trying to locate you there above, he'll survey the array of his teammates on the plane of the playing field, waiting; referee Yamasaki Maldonado will tell him to hurry up and, with one of his attacking teammates failing to get into position in their collective formation, he'll opt to go back on defense. But the bounce off the throw will get uncomfortable for Nilton Santos, so he'll fire it back past the rest of his team to start the progression over with their keeper, Gilmar. To you, it'll seem that, bored of the regressive actions on the pitch, we're cheering, trying to motivate the pawns to play, but what we're actually doing is protesting your mirror that dazzles without providing any warmth, without even revealing your face, and encouraging you to walk over to your fellow council members; wanting your plan to pick up pace; to get their keeper, Gilmar, to stop bouncing the ball on that grass that will be ours and to boot it hard; to have the ball sail across the pitch, clearing their side and searching for one of their forwards; but to have us be there, waiting, ready. We'll step up with the confident stride of Pluto Contreras and meet the ball before it lands, heading it to our teammate on the right, yes, the right: we'll send it to our wing, Ramírez Banda, and move with him in the opposite direction, toward the middle of the pitch, trying to break the same old circuit, sending a quick pass up to Honorino, revealing the form of our triangle, what our shape—not theirs and not that of the council of directors—is; and then we'll drop it back again to Eyzaguirre and make a run through the middle of their penalty area, but they won't let us see it, we'll combine with Eyzaguirre to reestablish the point of a shape that'll make the game more than a game, needing you to lower your mirror, we'll strike the ball too hard, driving it out of bounds behind the other team's goal. The important thing is that our shouts, our shrieking whistles, our thunderous applause will prompt you to think twice and to retrieve the coat you'd previously handed to the valet; better to put that object back in your pocket, that quicksilver or weapon or sharp blade, better to leave it there for now and only use it at the opportune moment.

So, without that reflection, the new goal kick from their keeper, Gilmar, will sail even higher, crossing the gray skies of the Campos de Sports and falling in the middle of our red half, where the head of Didí will find the ball first and send it to his teammate, Garrincha, always eluding us, like your face, and we'll pressure him with Raúl Sanchez, and ball will bounce out between us and the leg of Didí; but before we can move in with Eladio, Didí will strike the ball hard, sending it in a parabola to our left, where we'll stop it from going across the touchline with the feet of the guerrillero Rodríguez but will fail to swing it quickly over to Leonel because, before we can, Djalma Santos will cut it out and deliver it to Vavá, who will quickly touch it on to Didí, the former making a run so the latter can return him the ball in stride along touchline, meanwhile you'll have moved across the luxury box toward the awaiting banquet, and their pass will sail long, and the ball will roll slowly down the middle of the pitch toward our goal, and with those eyes, the eyes of Raúl Sánchez, our eyes, we'll watch the way you navigate the silver, leather, wood, and cashmere obstacles that appear in your path, and with the eyes of Raúl Sánchez we'll watch how with our keeper, Escuti, we pick up the ball, bounce it once, and put it back into play in the direction of Eyzaguirre, waiting downfield on the right, and seeing you walk by, a man in a dark suit, *sin vergüenza*, will set down his glass between seats with a stupefied expression, reddened eyes widening slightly, and reach his brazen hands out for your waist; with Eyzaguirre we'll pass the ball to our wing, Ramírez Banda, and continue our run through the middle while send a looping cross with our wing the width of the midfield line to the guerrillero Rodríguez on the opposite side, the left, and your fellow council member will say something shameless while sliding his fingers down to your hip; we'll opt to drop the ball back to Eladio, but the pass is imprecise and Didí will step up and take possession, preparing to read how his teammates are circulating: you'll know the impulse of those groping fingers well and will take another step to see how intense that collective intoxication is, and along the right touchline, Vavá will make a run, two strides; Didí will have pushed the ball out into space in front of him and will step up and strike it so hard that he'll slip, the *sin vergüenza* director will clumsily scramble to stand up to get his hands on your body as you elusively move to pin a piece of his suit to his seat, stepping on it with one foot, glass in hand, making him fall. Vavá will remain on the grass and you, our eyes, and the ball will be lost, wide of the mark, reds, whites, blues beyond the chalk endline; but the Uruguayan linesman will have raised his flag anyway. Offside, a man behind you will laugh. Too slow, another beside you will chuckle, motioning with one hand for the valets to help up the *sin vergüenza* in the three-piece suit.

For more than ten paces, we'll hold the ball in our keeper's gloves, and you'll move yours in what might be construed as a gesture of satisfaction, proceeding to the banquet table, the ball moving across the field again, and with our defender, Raúl Sánchez, we'll drop it back to Escuti, and give it another touch with him before sending a hard searching ball for Jorge Toro near midfield. Despite the chill in the afternoon air, you'll remove one of your gloves, an action that will allow you to evade the tall, gray-haired albino man approaching you, brandishing a pack of cigarettes.

Zito, tireless, incomprehensibly everywhere, will be in position to trap the dropping ball. You'll turn away, but he won't be deterred despite your insistence, back to us, though not to him; Zito will deliver the ball to Nilton Santos, but the imprecision of his execution will look like hesitation and their play will break down as we step up with Honorino to intercept the ball and cut down the right touchline, pursued by the long strides of Nilton Santos. In a blink, we'll suspend the battle for position on the pitch, our shape coming together all at once: you and the gray-haired albino will be speaking in a different language that we won't understand, the men near you in the luxury box won't either, much less the local directors, who will smile, eyes closed, dozing in their plush leather seats. We'll one-touch the ball to our wing, Ramírez Banda, stepping up together, two by two, our block of red shifting into a V: victorious or vanquished, our shape a vessel or a mountain peak. A triangle. The gray-haired albino will lift a hand up in front of your face and draw a line in the air, your head's momentum tracking both what he's drawing and this narration. We'll draw one of those converging lines with Ramírez Banda, touching the ball into space, tracing the other with Jorge Toro as we streak up to fire the ball from just outside their area, our hands executing both movements simultaneously until impact, our cheering, our shouting, *conchesumadre*, swelling because we're going to give it everything we've got with Jorge Toro. Our shouting, full-throated, will be like the ball that rises toward the goal, and you'll say something to the gray-haired albino as you remove one hand from your pocket and touch the leg of his pants; the ball will head for the goal and will be about to go in, but it won't bend, won't drop, missing just over the right side of the crossbar, and the gray-haired albino man won't give you another look, just hand you a cigarette, stand up, turn around, and walk furtively out into the hallway, through the vestibule, down the stairway, through the door to the luxury box, out the main entrance, across the parking lot, into taxi, bound for the airport, maybe, as the ball will be lost beyond the goal, through our cheers, our disappointed shouts of bad fucking luck, *mala suerte*, and *conchelalora*, and your hands will have returned to your coat pockets, as you stand there, cigarette in your mouth, staring, we think, at the space left empty beside you, beneath our feet, out on the field.

And up there on the scoreboard the Brazilian team will still be one goal ahead. We'll still be whistling behind your backs, behind your back, dear listener, and up in the luxury box, the director with the double moustache will still be calling to you from the banquet table, having just popped an ancient bottle to please his clean-shaven fellow council member, who will still be raising his glass in your direction. The opposing keeper, Gilmar, will still be setting the ball down inside their penalty area, stepping back, and booting it, while up in the stands we'll still be cheering for Jorge Toro, for Chile, for the goal that we're still trying to score, for you to turn around so we can recognize you. The ball will drop in the middle of our half and we'll step up to it with Raúl Sánchez, his back to Garrincha, and head it in search of a combination; we'll catch on with Jorge Toro and try to chip it back high, the ball will hang in the air and Didí won't be able to reach it, but we'll get there with Raúl Sánchez and one-touch it back to Jorge Toro in the center circle; the ball will have gone up in the air so many times that our eyes will remain fixed there above, on your long coat, seeing from behind how you'll button it back up to protect yourself from the cold, how you'll rest your elbows on the bar by the banquet table, and how you'll stay there, waiting for the director with the double moustache and his fellow director with the champagne, one of your hands always in your pocket. *Vamos miércale*, fucking hell, let's go, we'll still be cheering. We'll head it again with Jorge Toro toward Pluto Contreras on the right side of our half and touch it quickly on to Eyzaguirre and then over to our wing, Ramírez Banda; we'll celebrate the sequence of passes that clarify the drawing of our attacking shape, swept along by the drawing of your gloved hands as they glide across the spotless bar tracking what you're hearing over the luxury box loudspeaker: we'll advance with our wing, Ramírez Banda, but then turn and drop the ball back to Jorge Toro, possessing the ball and running with him, not wanting to disrupt our flow down the left flank with a pass, even though your gloved hand will move in the opposite direction as the barman offers you a *vaina* cocktail and one of the council members who's been feigning directorial inebriation at the banquet table will turn around to admire you, standing at the bar, from behind; we'll still be advancing with Jorge Toro, when suddenly Garrincha's right foot will come in from behind and cut off our path before we can elude Didí, fouling us, as referee Yamasaki Maldonado and his whistle will indicate immediately. Then we'll stop the ball on the grass with Leonel's hands, our red shirts dispersing across the green, inverting our triangle, because now we've found the name of our strategy; as the canarinho team forms a single defensive rectangle, man to man, we'll back up with our striker and start running toward the ball, eyes staring straight ahead and not up. Listen: what does the clean-shaven man whisper to you as he sets his glass of whiskey on the bar, because he stares straight ahead and not directly at you as he speaks. Listen: the others, our rival comrades, will expect a direct kick at the elusive goal, or at least a looping ball into the middle of their penalty area, but we'll send a hard and driven pass to the far left side of the pitch; your gloved hand, the one not in your pocket, will react by moving the glass of *vaina* away from those ruddy groping fingers; we'll be posted up on the left with the guerrillero Rodríguez and will attempt to continue the zigzag combination with him, but Didí will slide in with both feet and knock the ball away from us and into an area where Djalma Santos can retrieve it and jog into space, looking for his teammates to reconfigure their familiar formation. And yet, we'll notice a new detail, that those ruddy fingers won't insolently try to intertwine with your gloved ones but instead will slip a piece of paper into your palm. A check. We'll know them now. The pass to Vavá won't work, the ball will bounce out into the middle and we'll alter its trajectory with Eladio, touching it deftly over to Jorge Toro, with whom we'll cross it the width of the pitch to Eyzaguirre and make a slashing vertical run with him as you remove your left hand from your pocket, bring it down to your other hand, rip the check cleanly into four pieces, and throw it to the ground; we'll cheer for all of it and for the pass that we'll send with Eyzaguirre to our wing, Ramírez Banda, on the right, close enough to their penalty area now that our frontline sees the opportunity, that we launch the ball into the middle of the danger area and dive with our center forward, Tobar, to direct it on frame, getting tangled in the effort with the extremities of Zito as he moves in to try and clear the ball from the area, and we'll get confused and won't understand the movement of the clean-shaven council member up in the luxury box as he struggles to his feet and furrows his brow, whether he's clumsily trying to take his glass of whiskey with him or to throw it at you or to shove it, rudely, at the barman, gesturing for him to refill it, and we'll fall; the ball will bounce on the penalty marker in the opponent's box and just graze Zózimo as our collective red shape presses in and we step up with Eladio to strike the ball, time and place aligning entirely in our favor. Our strike will be fierce; your gloved left hand will return to your pocket. Why might the clean-shaven man have feigned drunken clumsiness only to threaten you when he's been running his own business in these regions for decades? The opposing keeper, Gilmar, will stretch out in vain, and the ball will go in, *puta la hueá*, oh fuck, but no; it'll thunder off the right post. The ball will bounce back out into the penalty area, right to our feet; and the entire stadium, eighty thousand of us, will step up with Jorge Toro to strike it again; you'll leap to your feet and shake the clean-shaven man by his shoulders and, before stepping back, a minor insult he had coming, adjust the tie, hair, vest, and cufflinks of that odious director, who will scramble to his feet and immediately ask his valet the location of the bathroom; everyone in the stadium will step up with Jorge Toro to strike the ball again and, blind, nervous, inaccurate, rip a shot wide of that open net.

Now the Brazilian team will reconfigure their two blocks into a solid shape that contains us, at least that's what their keeper, Gilmar, will hope, sending a searching ball for Djalma Santos, racing down our left side to the rhythm of a high-pitched screech that'll yank our eyes upward: they'll have brought a ringing telephone out into the luxury box, listen, it's ringing for you. Gilmar's goal kick won't reach its target, finding Leonel's feet instead, and we'll make a play on the ball with him and run after it when we fail to contain its bounce—the ringing telephone and the eyes of the man with the double moustache—and Mauro Ramos will get there first and send it back onto our side of the pitch in a parabola that'll drop right to Garrincha. Why are you still standing at the bar? What are you waiting for? Garrincha, on the other hand, won't wait, running away from the pressure of Eladio and Jorge Toro, together, independent, opening up space: we'll hear someone else answer the telephone in that out-of-reach luxury box, we'll let Didí trap the ball and notice the gap between their wings along the border of the pitch, and set up our red shirts to watch their trap develop, that combination where Vavá will slash through the middle toward the goal, our focal point, but no; Vavá will dribble the ball with no clear aim beyond contrasting his canarinho shirt with our green grass, marred, desiccated, withered, yellow in the end, and you'll glance up because someone will be saying your name through the noise, what is it?; fucking hell, we won't catch it. Didí will send a long pass back to Vavá who will step up to take us on directly and we won't know whether to challenge him with our keeper, Escuti, or to wait—what is the name the valet carrying the Bakelite telephone across the luxury box said?—but they won't give us time or space. We'll be too slow and too far away as we move out to challenge Vavá with Escuti, forcing him to strike the ball quickly and fuck, *por la rechucha*, another goal, but no: referee Yamasaki Maldonado will have blown his whistle, barely audible amid our cries of relief and recrimination; fucking *saco de huea*, took him long enough, why were they making you wait and not alerting you that you had a phone call? Why won't he say your name? When the referee whistles the play dead, we'll let the players get back from their offside position; you'll have gotten up from the bar to keep the long telephone cord from getting wrapped around your foot as you take the apparatus, covering the mouthpiece for a second. You won't want to speak yet or at least won't want to stop watching how, following the infraction, we put the ball back into play with Pluto Contreras, sending it up to our keeper, Escuti, and how we kick it with him hard to the right, up to the middle of our half where it'll skip and bounce up to the chest of Jorge Toro, with whom, however, we won't be able to control it, and it'll be recovered by the opposing forward, Amarildo, who will get support from his teammate, Zagallo, touching the pass right to him, and up in the luxury box they'll leave the telephone there for you to speak at your leisure. Then Zagallo will accelerate toward our red area, but first we'll interpret the circulation between the two, your hand on the receiver, Pluto's leg with which we'll deflect a quick pass to Honorino, and moving quickly with him we'll approximate the shape that we'll only have been able to draw across the field a few times: an open pass to our wing, Ramírez Banda, already making a run; we'll keep running with him, leaving Nilton Santos behind, and the receiver will remain there, inert on the bar in front of you for as long as the cigarette that you'll light burns, listening to us on the transistor radios. We won't all be on board for Honorino to pass the ball to Ramírez Banda; so, we'll pull up and drop it back a few meters to Jorge Toro and pause with him too, the ball at our feet, waiting to confirm that you won't pick up the telephone, that our plural attacking shape will crystallize, that all of us will find a way to see each other simultaneously, waiting to blink and send the ball back to Honorino. We'll make a turn with him along the edge of the canarinho area as Zózimo will come sliding in with both feet up to send the ball in the opposite direction. Listen: exhale all the smoke from your cigarette and touch the receiver with one gloved finger, leave it there, lying on the lacquered surface of the bar, where another valet, with an expression of concern, will offer you a glass of water. From the receiver, you'll hear an incessant voice: answer it, answer us; confirm that you'll do what you've come to do; don't tell us your name; don't turn toward the crowd, if we never see your face we'll be able to ignore who's responsible for what's going to happen; later, we'll fully erase your presence: the ball will drop into the center circle once again, but now the canarinho forward won't get to it, because we'll hold our position with Pluto and possess it. You would've recognized our shape even if you weren't carefully depositing your cigarette ash on the lacquered surface of the bar to illustrate everything that we're telling you: that we'll pass the ball to Raúl Sánchez, that our offensive organization will maintain that shape, even if it has no impact on the result. Because this will never stop being a game, listen. Because we'll send a long pass to Honorino on our right, to turn this flashing glance into a comprehensive view; with him we'll calmly run down that touchline, leaving Zagallo behind with a single fake, going right at Didí and before they can take the ball, we'll pass it to our wing, Ramírez Banda, waiting with him for a teammate to send it to, and glimpsing in your cigarette ash that our triangle will have become an arrow. We'll cross the backline they've imposed on us with Honorino and take ownership of the opposing area; we'll feel the ball on our feet, even as it rises through the air, even as we mistake its leather opacity for the orb of the sun, disappearing behind the winter clouds, and even as it bounces to Nilton Santos, who will seize the moment and send it away, skimming across the ground along the same right touchline but in the opposite direction; even as you stub out your cigarette without apologizing to the barman for the lines of ash you've left on the lacquered surface, holding the receiver in your gloved hand for a moment: you'll weigh the voice that insists that you respond, you'll listen to ours that tells you how badly we want to reach that ball before it's lost, battling Zagallo with Eyzaguirre to control it, your hand a knot on the receiver; please, don't answer. And yet: one phrase, just one. That's all you'll say into the telephone, very quickly, before hanging up: neither them nor us. We'll have gotten Eyzaguirre tangled up with Zagallo and will lose the ball out into touch.

Then you'll stay there, hands folded on the bar, you won't even glance at the telephone that'll ring again two, three more times before going definitively silent. You'll stay still, listening to us, and down on the field, the whistle will ring out for you too: the moment to act will have come. Nilton Santos will throw the ball in to their other forward, Amarildo, in the center, who will get control of it just as we come up behind him to take it away with Raúl Sán-chez. But we won't have anywhere to turn with it, so we'll just send it back out over the touchline. Zito will take the throw this time, sending it high and hard to Zagallo; he'll head it to their forward, Amarildo, once again, and once again you'll leave your gloved left hand on top of the pack of cigarettes on the bar, your right hand in your pocket. There, your back turned, we'll know you'll have been listening to us, waiting for the right moment. We'll go on defense to disrupt their flow, stepping up with Pluto Contreras to cut out the ball and one-touch it to Eladio in the center circle, as the field opens up into the shape of a red triangle interposed in their block of pressing canarinho shirts and, stepping on the ball with Eladio, we'll change everything's direction, shifting to the right; you'll re-move your gloved hand from that pocket once again, examining the piece of paper that you put there before, while tapping on the lacquered surface of the bar with your hand, marking a beat, sig-naling that your fellow council members will want us to continue to the right, but what about you? We'll go that way anyway, be-cause Vavá's pressure won't leave us an option. Continuing our run across the width of the pitch with Eladio, we'll turn to send a pass back, on our heels now even though we're losing by a goal to the world champions, pay attention: to elude the man with the double moustache who will come walking over to the bar, you'll let your-self drop in one of the luxury box's plush leather seats, just one more among the dozens of dozing directors. Then we'll quickly shift the run we're making to the left, surprising our pursuer and, in so doing, the shape we've been trying to find will advance in this game of yours and of theirs, as we break in a straight line down the middle of the pitch with Eladio, unexpectedly the seat to your left will remain vacant and the man with the double moustache, watching you now from a distance, his brow furrowed against the sudden glare of the winter sun, won't be able to take you by the arm as he planned; no doubt he'll have brought an accounting book in his briefcase, where he'll have drawn up numbers that'll yield more profits for the business his family has been running for centuries across many countries under the façade of democracy, civil justice, penal systems, political and—for a few years now—sports culture, and so, without missing a beat, he'll snap his fingers to get the valet to bring him an even pricier bottle of champagne. We'll keep running with Eladio in a straight line down the center of the field, elongating the triangle with a quick pass on the ground to Honorino, angling right with him, the ball glued to our instep, accelerating toward their goal, open for others, and then motherfucker, *chuchamadre*; Mauro Ramos will force that cry out of us, leg high, cleats cutting into our calf, even though we'll have managed to deliver the ball to our wing, Ramírez Banda, first; the plush leather seat next to you must remain vacant, even though the circuit will already be in motion, unceasing; from our wing we'll send it to our center forward, Tobar, and cut with him toward the corner on the other left side of the other team, opponents and comrades. You'll rest your head on the seatback and we'll imagine that you close your eyes so you'll only hear these words, not seeing us when we don't see you: in the face of the men pressing in around you, you'll cling to the certainty that, as with your ancestors, they'll erase your name from this story, that your face and body and figure won't be part of the council of directors, of the booing fans, of the players on the field, but will be part of the game; which is why none of them will come sit beside you yet, waiting instead at the banquet table and the bar, without hurry but with greater conviction than you. That's what they'll think and that is for the best, because in the movement of your fingers across your forehead, we'll see that you've decided to accelerate your plan, to carry it out before halftime: your goal will be to carry our hopes and dreams beyond the game; to find a way to turn us into repetition, to turn permanence into anguish, and finally to turn this anxiety of complementary time into infinite anodyne narration, this feeling that a victory for us will be as attainable as it is chimerical, that once and for all we'll be able to articulate a closing, a cut, a finale for all of this, the culmination of this string of words that'll never be entirely ours; thereafter we'll want to say that all together we're only at our best in our drunken revelry, at our matches, and in the literature we'll pass down to our progeny; with any luck we'll find a way to plot a novel where eighty thousand, eight hundred, eight million of us will take first place, and only then be awarded an overflowing cup that will immediately be taken away on a golden tray and delivered to another director up there in the luxury box whom we can't see. Your fellow council members will take it for us. And at that point, the concrete reality of our booing will escape us, because the imagination, the ability to say this, the very possibility of stating that we're switching roles is also controlled by the directors right now on this very radio broadcast, just screams that we'll scream because we retrieve the ball with our center forward, Tobar, near the flag in the opposing team's corner. And listen carefully: under pressure from Nilton Santos, our shape will draw a disciplined line, piercing their open and distant area; we won't even need to look up at you, already knowing that we'll all be moving together through the middle of the opponent's penalty area, turning defense into offense, and we'll leave the canarinho defender behind once and for all with our center forward, Tobar, making a cut and sending a cross at a right angle while leaping off the ground with Honorino to meet it, holy fuck, *chetumare*, his right leg trailing slightly behind the left to strike it out of midair, *chetumá, una chilenita*, a bicycle kick crossways of the goalmouth, yes; their keeper will be frozen and the ball will go in, but fuck, no, *por la rechuchetumare*; it'll sail wide to the right and be lost in the cacophony, in the stands, not of a roar but of a groan, and your hands will come together in a single clap, still one to zero, and two claps won't get you to open your eyes to witness our acrobatics.

Their lucky keeper, Gilmar, will quickly get things going again from in front of the goal, sending a hard strike all the way to the center circle where we'll leap up with Jorge Toro to battle Amarildo for it, but our opponent will win the ball and flick it on to his teammate, Zito, deeper in our half; you still won't open your eyes: their runs will be vertical lines, streaking down field, because as the canarinho center forward, Amarildo, continues running after making the pass, Zito will send the ball back to him, and he'll slash through our red shirts, finding the space between us, dispersed, looking up and seeing that your back is still turned. So, none of our red shirts will get there, for fuck's sake; Amarildo will cut goalward at a diagonal through our unlucky area that we're always trying to escape and strike it toward the right corner, but not in, because fucking hell, we'll dive to the left, head and arms leading the way, with our keeper, Escuti, in time to block the shot with our cheering and the ball will bounce, shrieking, back out to us. We'll possess it with Eladio at the top of our danger area, but they'll still be pressing hard, this time with their other forward, Garrincha, trying to take another shot, despite Eladio, who with our whistles, choked cries, and shins we'll use to defend and protect the ball until we fall silent and hear the whistle of the referee, Yamasaki Maldonado, stopping play because, to him, our tackle on Garrincha was especially savage: crooked, paid-off *saquero* ref, *madre, hijo*, we'll continue insulting him; false brother, treacherous Peruvian neighbor. Then you'll open your eyes. Our wave of curses will blur the lines of our coalescing shape and propel you out of your plush leather seat. We'll line up six red shirts inside our penalty area to cover the free kick, giving instructions with Escuti: a reddish line transversing the withered green will be all that's left of our effaced shape, a wall, please, look at us, out here facing down the canarinho arrow at whose base Didí, Garrincha, and Amarildo are deciding who will take the kick and whip the ball into this net that is ours but will never belong to us. To the left, farther left, for fuck's sake, intensity rising in the stands. You'll remain on your feet, listening, registering our insults; finally, without even stepping back, Didí will strike the ball along the ground—wake up!—so hard that it'll go right past one side of our wall and roll harmlessly across the endline at the edge of our area, far from anyone's goal. You'll have understood: our goal is to have everything start with defense; Brazil's goal is to attack to avoid defending. Your aim will be to rupture any impulse to attack or defend, to eliminate opposition in order to leave your fellow council members out there in the middle, directing, believing they're dictating what to do but ignorant of the fact that without dichotomy, without separating themselves from us, we won't see or hear them. And so, in the end, us, them, and our opponents will all be deprived of our objective, the opposing goal, and nobody will have told us about the abolition of that basic rule of the game: now we'll entertain ourselves running away from the center circle, believing we can escape that magnet.

You'll remain standing, knowing your fellow council members up there in the luxury box won't come to you if you don't seem to want to come to them. We'll hurry the goal kick with our keeper, Escuti, over to our wing, Ramírez Banda, on the touchline, and with him we'll drop the ball back to Eyzaguirre on the right and continue jogging down the touchline to reestablish our red triangle shape that we'll be hoping to draw with greater clarity. But our triangle will start turning into a funnel behind the field's center circle, so with our wing, Ramírez Banda, we'll retreat from the pressure of Zagallo coming for the ball with such speed that we'll be forced to send the ball much farther back, along the ground, all the way to our keeper, Escuti, with whom we'll pick it up and look out at how the triangle, the funnel, the mountain peak is warping into an as-yet nameless polyhedric shape, and then, once again, it'll appear to us as a V, victory for someone on the field, vengeance for you, vanity for everyone, if not vestige, void, a more open V, our palms coming together in applause, but your gloved hands will remain closed under your coat as you start walking over to the banquet table, better to wrap our keeper's hands around the ball, holding it against our chest, one of your gloves atop the other in two concentric fists: we'll see that, but not your face, turned away. We'll bounce the ball and punt it hard up the right touchline with Escuti, trapping it with the feet of our wing, Ramírez Banda, as the referee blows play dead for a foul on Zito; he'll have come out of nowhere, his foot colliding with our shin. We'll set the ball on the ground with our wing, Ramírez Banda, and take the free kick, sending it up ahead to Jorge Toro and cutting left with Ramírez Banda to find our shape: listen, with the blinking eyes of Jorge Toro, we'll consider combinations that'll never present themselves; we'll pause briefly before delivering a high ball to the top of the distant canarinho area where we'll be calling for it with Honorino and then as we turn to make a run—what the fuck!, *por la cresta*, hey ref, you piece of shit, Peruvian neighbor, fingernail of my fingernail—we'll go off the handle because Zito will slide in and tackle us from behind, but our boos and heckling will quickly turn to cheering as Yamasaki Maldonado blows his whistle to award us a free kick, but a simulation; up in the luxury box, looking down at the banquet table, you'll reach out one gloved hand and touch the tablecloth, a gesture that appears hesitant, disoriented, once again attracting the immediate attention of the man with the double moustache. With the foot of our wing, Ramírez Banda, we'll send the indirect kick to Jorge Toro and run with him down that right touchline, out on the pitch where days before your fellow council members gathered to discuss plans for the social development of the sport; the man with the double moustache will follow you with his eyes, with your back turned you'll use your gloved left hand to indicate to a valet what to put on your plate, and we'll run through another repetition of the V shape with Jorge Toro, after blinking and considering the same intangible combinations. So, we'll step up, pause briefly, and then send a high ball to the top of that distant canarinho area where we'll be making a run with Honorino; our wave of cheering will be his run, a player of such power, and then the booing and cries of recrimination that—motherfucking *putamadre*, treacherous brother, scum of scum, *piñen de mi piñen*—we'll unleash after losing the battle with Zózimo and falling to the ground, even though we'll know that it's all a simulation, what you're doing and what the referee who this time won't blow his whistle, Yamasaki Maldonado, is doing. Trying to catch us off guard, the canarinho keeper will quickly take the goal kick, sending it all the way to the center circle where we'll continue drawing our shape across the pitch with Raúl Sánchez, heading it back into the attacking end; making a run with Eladio we'll trap it and try to send a pass to our center forward, Tobar, but no, you'll reach out to take the cutlery and canapés from the hands of the valet with an affectation of fragility, hesitation, because in that way you'll get the man with the double moustache to step in, smiling, and take them for you and, for a moment, you'll stop listening to how we'll fail to trap the ball with the feet of our center forward, Tobar, because Zito will anticipate the play and cut the ball out, but in vain: the ball will roll away without anyone gaining possession, the man with the double moustache will finally have your plate in his hands, and then we'll track it down with the feet of a streaking Jorge Toro, advancing toward their area, chased by Didí and Zito; at the same time, you will turn your back on us, walking slowly over to the luxury box bar, where more valets will be waiting to serve you more drinks, and with our back to Zito we'll push up, but again, no, fuck me, *conchamimadre*: book him already ref, *señor árbitro* Yamasaki Maldonado, name of your name, will blow his whistle because the opposing player will have slid in and tackled us illegally once again.

Simulating too, you'll avoid letting your fingers touch the tray, the cutlery, the three forks, the four glasses filled with sparkling water, white wine, red wine, and some other liquid that not even those of us in the radio broadcast booth know the name of. So we'll crowd four of our red shirts together in the green center at the top of their area, walking with one of our forwards toward the right corner of the pitch, while their defense will take the form of a wall of five canarinho players and one floating free inside the area we're hoping to attack, all of them watching our wing, Ramírez Banda, with whom we'll move toward the corner and yet, listen, he'll end up on the other side: with your left hand you'll lean on the bar and start to remove your glove; we'll be setting up for the kick with Leonel, picking up the ball, setting it down at our feet, and continuing to converse with Jorge Toro, while the referee, Yamasaki Maldonado, will demand, through the encouraging murmur of our voices, that the wall our opponents have formed not move until he blows the whistle, at which point we won't take the direct shot with Leonel that our opponents are anticipating, instead we'll open up and swing it in diagonally to our wing, Ramírez Banda, and then all of us will spread out into our formations, you'll remove your second glove with the slowness necessary to make the man with the double moustache have to stand there and watch the friction of leather against skin, the red attacking arrow and our bases at both edges of the opposing area will crystallize for us, and at the same time their funnel, canarinho-yellow over the green-yellow of the grass, withered each morning by winter, will form a solid foundation and a curving line of five players between the corners of the semicircle at the top of the box. With the run of our wing, Ramírez Banda, we'll rupture the expected flow of the shapes, and you'll do the same: with intentional clumsiness, you'll drop your left glove and wait for the man with the double moustache to bend gallantly down in his drunkenness to retrieve it; instead of proceeding toward our sideline, we'll make a quick cut to the middle with our wing, anticipating that the line of our arrow shape will be drawn by a vertical run with Eladio, so we'll drop the ball into space in front of him where he can put it on goal and he'll strike it with power, goddamn it, but without aim; when you let the glove slip from your fingers and the man with the double moustache bends down to retrieve it, we won't know in that moment if he was already collapsing, but you'll react reflexively and in less than a second snatch your glove out of the air with your other hand; we'll send the ball out across the endline, wide of their goal; with the inertia of that empty trajectory you'll make the man with the double moustache fall dramatically at your feet with a clatter of trays, dishes, food, silverware, and glasses; a collision that you'll escape the way you escape our eyes, indistinguishable among the rush of valets and directors who will jump to their feet to assist the poor bastard. By the time the opposing keeper, Gilmar, puts the ball back into play from his area, by the time he steps back, surveys the pitch, accelerates, and delivers the goal kick, up in the luxury box, the uptight directors will already have congregated to settle their business dealings with the body of the man with the double moustache, prostrate on the floor. Valets will have fetched smelling salts, glasses of water, a siphon of medicinal whiskey, and the shape of your body will have vanished in the crowd, turning your back on us. The goal kick will once again sail across midfield and drop on our half of the pitch, colliding with the head of Pluto Contreras, but no; one of their player's heads will get to it first, the head of their striker, Amarildo, who will proceed to trap the ball with his right foot and touch it back to Vavá who will pull up and send it to his teammate, Zagallo, on our right, and the two great shapes will be clearly drawn across the pitch as you disappear into the crowd of scandalized council members: the canarinho H will push up across the withered grasses while our red funnel will contract; looking to their wing, Zagallo, the rest of the team will have perceived the shift, and he'll send a driven ball along the ground to the edge of the area that appears to be ours, the area into which Amarildo will run with the ball until we cut him off with the outstretched foot of Raúl Sánchez, with whom we'll accelerate up the right touchline, waiting for our funnel to become an arrow and to once again glimpse your silhouette among the dark suits of the directors. We'll pause now along the chalk touchline with Raúl Sánchez, looking down the pitch and sending a long searching ball in the direction of Honorino, with whom we'll have entered the opposing area, but they'll beat us to it, leaping up with Zózimo and sending it back up into the air, undeterred, we'll head their rebuttal with our wing, Ramírez Banda, to Eyzaguirre, a play that won't pan out for us because Didí will cut the ball out and make a run, initiating the next canarinho combination: an ellipsis; wherever you are that we can't see, you'll be listening; better, their elliptical shape will start to come together with a pass to their other forward, Garrincha, who will run to receive it in space and send it back to Djalma Santos, who will deliver it to Vavá in a parallel position, where he'll find an angle that'll allow him to pass the ball back to Garrincha. But first, yes, we'll read the pattern with the guerrillero Rodríguez and anticipate it, stepping up to intercept the pass, realizing that the shape we'll want to trace across the withered grasses of our winter is no longer a V but a T: later, sooner, a reversible T will still be better, a T that'll flow through the one player of ours who will continue through the center of their ignored area; we'll keep pushing up with the guerrillero Rodríguez, cutting diagonally to the inside, rupturing the structure of the competition and emerging into a space where the only option will be to face down their goal, to look up and shoot: crush it, *compadre*, but no, the ball will roll harmlessly a few meters wide of the goal post; not even a trace of your back in that wall of navy blue, gray, and black jackets, blazers, sweaters, sport coats, frock coats, liveries, houppelandes, doublets, scarves, windbreakers, *americanas*, overcoats, shirts, topcoats, hunting jackets, dolmans, raincoats, macfarlanes, mackintoshes, gaberdines, soutanes, pullovers, button-downs, shirtfronts, ruffles, ties, cravats, bowties, kerchiefs, T-shirts, tracksuits, suspenders, top hats, galoshes, boots, socks, stockings, slippers, long underwear, and short trousers that swirl around accompanied by hands holding glasses, champagne flutes, wine glasses, snifters, and shot glasses all clustering together around the man with the double moustache who will remain prostrate on the floor of the luxury box. So, their keeper, Gilmar, will take another goal kick and the ball will sail high across the pitch to the center circle where we'll head it back in the opposite direction with Jorge Toro but then lose it to the feet of the opposing wing, Zagallo; we'll make a play on the ball with Eladio but fail to keep Didí from possessing it in the center circle where we'll collide with him and fall to the ground. And yet, we'll get back up protecting the ball with our body; our red clustering around, waiting, yelling at the referee, Yamasaki Maldonado, to blow play dead because Didí touched the ball with his hand, but no: one of your fellow council members will tell a joke, eliciting a burst of laughter from the group of navy suits in the luxury box, who won't take their lips off their drinks or their hands off their briefcases, while four valets, pale amid the laughter, will keep checking the pulse of the man with the double moustache and carefully tending to him on the floor. Not a shadow of you anywhere. Whereas the other team will anticipate with Didí that we're attempting to trace a new collective formation, shifting our triangle shape into something we understand better; so they'll seize the moment to send a long ball directly to Amarildo at the point of their shape, and we'll go to the ground to battle him for the ball so aggressively with Pluto Contreras that now, yes, what the fuck!, *ahueonao*, *padre de tu padre*, Yamasaki Maldonado will blow his whistle and call a foul on us and their other forward will come to a quick stop; for a solemn second, we'll wait for you to appear behind the flushed group of pot-bellied, bald, big-toothed directors who will keep shrieking with laughter and silencing our breath, our curses, our cheers, but no: Amarildo's indirect free kick will become a long pass to Zagallo on our right, who will take off running with the ball to set up the canarinho team's H on the withered yellow grass, humid, humoral, humorous, different shades of the same winter burn; the joke of another of your fellow council members and subsequent laughter will shake the luxury box, variations distorting the snorts, chirps, and pants with which the Brazilian team will have moved across the pitch, not needing to shout to each other between touches, runs, and long balls which they'll weave together in the air without mockery, and in the uproar your indecipherable strategy for keeping your face hidden will have escaped us too. So you won't appear now either, but listen to us— even if only on a radio crackling up in that luxury box—as we rage:

wake up fuckhead *huevetas!*, we'll shout when the mismatch of our red shirts within the other team's H formation will become obvious in the middle of the area that's no longer ours; focused with our wing, Ramírez Banda, we'll try to get the ball away from Zagallo, who will dodge and weave, back and forth, the ball on his feet, making space for himself along the most advanced vertical line of their H and then send a high cross over the whole box to the opposite endpoint of that line, Garrincha, always attacking from our left. The defensive coverage on that side will, as usual, be shouldered by the guerrillero Rodríguez, with support from Leonel and Raúl Sánchez, closing in gradually; Garrincha will toy with us. We'll come right at him with both of the guerrillero's feet, but he'll fake us out and leave us lying on the ground, and when we bring more pressure with Raúl Sánchez, he'll pull back, make a quick cut, and dribble around us, leaving him on the ground too; get in the game, dumbass *pelotudos!*; the man with the double moustache will still be lying inert on the floor, whereas we'll go to the ground with Leonel to prevent the unfathomable Garrincha from advancing further and at least bring him down with a tackle that, of course, will draw an immediate whistle. Our admirable opponent's free kick, along our left flank, just outside the chalk border of our area, will be taken by Garrincha himself: a looping ball into the middle where the canarinho team will have moved into a triangle shape, a fleeting improvement on the one we'd failed to form ourselves a few minutes before, an attacking triangle with Amarildo in the middle, Vavá and Zagallo on either side and slightly back. Following Garrincha's free kick, the ball will bounce untouched by us, the home team, *La Roja*, red flesh of an open wound; though you might already have abandoned the luxury box, you'll still hear how the suits will now be taken aback by the red spectacle that has suddenly issued forth from the body of their fellow director on the floor of the luxury box. The ball will keep bouncing and we'll fail to control it with Eladio, even as we'll leap up to play it in the air with his foot; they won't trap it with Amarildo and neither will we, getting?? a second chance with Pluto Contreras; we'll finally take possession with Eyzaguirre and start jogging in the direction of the opposing team's half, slow enough to recompose a formation that isn't just the irregular defensive shape imposed upon us, some of the directors in the luxury box will hold up kerchiefs not of felt but of silk and pocket squares not of red jute but of satin to cover their mouths upon seeing that red liquid flow out of the unconscious body of their fellow council member. We'll escape with Eyzaguirre, sending the ball to Jorge Toro, distracted by your absence, running too far, because we'll be unable to locate you among the group of pale, mocking directors, and so Didí will get ahead of us and disrupt our flow; with his strike, the ball will come all the way back to the semicircle at the top of the red area that we'll never escape. We'll be waiting there with Raúl Sánchez, yes: for a long time, we'll have known how to defend, we'll have learned how to clear the ball, how to cut off the attacking flow of any foreign invasion here, assuming we have a goal to protect; and only based on that assumption will we ever initiate the possibility of an offensive convergence. We'll pass the ball to the right, easy for us in this part of the pitch, to Eyzaguirre, with whom we'll cut back to the middle and elude one, two opposing players, getting past the center circle and glimpsing an arrow opening up along the same circuit in the direction of our wing, Ramírez Banda; at the same time, among the grimaces of the monochrome group of suits, navy blue, beige, black, the gray-haired albino will reappear, tall and without a tie, chrome-colored in the last rays of the winter sun that's turning its back on our cordillera now, transforming into dust, fog, smoke until tomorrow.

The gray-haired albino will give a single twirl of his white-gold-ringed index finger and the group of suits will begin to disperse, to move away from the inert, red-leaking body on the luxury box's floor; the group will be in the shape of an arrow; with our wing, Ramírez Banda, we'll see the head of the arrow running to the right, ambitious, Honorino. We'll control the ball with Honorino, turning to confront the defensive line that'll begin with Nilton Santos and just as we're about to make the pass, he'll get his instep on the ball and send it back to our side of the pitch, where their other wing, Zagallo, will be making a run: our right side will be our most vulnerable flank and also where we make our best advances; we won't resign ourselves to your figure, your shape, your body having disappeared, to you having escaped, listen; we won't yet understand that all of us can form a single shape on these fields, but we will understand that Zagallo has begun to accelerate, glimpsing the edge of the second line of their H extending from his feet; and he'll keep running even though his eyes will be looking up at the other points of their formation. Beside him, Vavá. And instinctively we'll know that you'll be able to see this from above, without our narration: we're going to compress the red funnel, vibrating against the distinct shades of withered grass and canarinho players; wherever you are, you'll realize that, however crude it is, our funnel will stop them, so Zagallo will turn around and send the ball back along his vertical line to Zito. Just as the formation is complex and the milling irrational, you'll notice that up in the luxury box a single clap of the chrome-colored hands of the gray-haired albino will suffice to completely disband the wall of suits, though not the spate of ridicule for everything still under their feet; so that, symmetrically, Amarildo will appear in that area, red again, ours, an unmarked center forward, transverse line of that H, human, haze, hacienda, and will receive a quick and direct pass from Zito so that he can touch it right back to him for the death blow. But our field remains rough, soft, uneven, and the ball will take an unexpected bounce, skipping just enough so that Jorge Toro can steal it and send it out to Leonel, with whom we'll touch it right back to him and cut over to the opposite side of their dissolving shape, while on the ball with Jorge Toro we'll accelerate across midfield. At which point we'll pause for a moment, waiting for something to appear on our horizon: a collective shape to converge into, but we'll opt to send it out to the right point, where we've been moving ceaselessly with our wing, Ramírez Banda, bringing together that part of the arrow that'll promise a gleam distinct from the gleam of the winter sun, of the canarinho shirts, and of the gold on the hand of the gray-haired albino up in the luxury box, a gleam of our own tones, red, bloody, cupreous. With our wing, Ramírez Banda, we'll carry the ball diagonally to the edge of the opposing area where we'll leave it for Honorino, switching positions: the structure will be plural for us, now that there above your fellow council members have moved away from the spectacle of the body on the floor; we'll also have understood with our clever *compadre*, Honorino, where the rest of our teammates are headed, and we'll send a long searching ball through their area, but this time Mauro Ramos will be faster, slipping in and deflecting it with his heel into space for Nilton Santos, in front of our opponent's corner flag. We'll be stunned here in the stands when Santos sends it quickly back down our right side, because with nothing more than that rushed defensive clearance, they'll have drawn a pentagonal shape with a left side that will overwhelm our right, the pass landing at the feet of their wing, Zagallo, who, advancing toward our wing, Ramírez Banda, won't yet have a way to follow the line that cuts downfield and to the middle. So, as they drop the ball back to Nilton Santos, a yawn will escape one of your fellow council members, plopped down in one of the plush leather seats in the luxury box; whereas, under pressure from Honorino, their defender will flick the ball into the air and step adroitly around us, continuing to press ahead: and in that moment we'll realize that they're going to break down their previous shape and construct a new one, indecipherable to us; they'll be looking for a new triangle, we'll think, when they deliver a different kind of ball to their forward, Amarildo. We still won't see you but will be able to step up with Raúl Sánchez and steal the ball anyway, initiating a different trajectory, but not before referee Yamasaki Maldonado, unsuspected neighbor, will call what to his blind eyes was a foul committed previously by Nilton Santos on Honorino. We'll spread out across the withered grass, make sweeping runs, and simulate putting the ball into play with an indirect kick from Pluto Contreras to our wing, Ramírez Banda, with whom we'll possess the ball, covering a long stretch of the pitch, looking for the next link and finding it in a distinct shape: two rectangular blocks with our wing connecting along a perpendicular line to Jorge Toro, connecting in turn to our block of center forwards, despite the fact that Zito will be all over us, preventing us from knowing whether our collective movement is crowd noise, harmony, or pure imagination. Then, we'll briefly suppress the collective impulse with Jorge Toro, erasing the team, we'll stop looking for your face up there in the luxury box and go straight at that familiar goal that we want so badly to score on. So we'll fire a driven ball from outside the box, fuck; with all our power, my soul, this small chest, these arms, this breath, and all our hoarse shrieks, motherfucking *conchetumadre*, we'll pull Jorge Toro's foot back and drive it forward, striking the ball; the ball will rise, bound for an upper corner when their keeper, *desgraciado* Gilmar, will leap up out of nowhere and block our shot and our cheers.

We'll hurry the corner kick with Leonel, making a short pass to the guerrillero Rodríguez, who will send it back as we consolidate a formation of four red shirts within the canarinho funnel that'll be protecting the opposing area, enticing for a moment and yes, now: though a couple of your fellow council members cheer too, behind them others with big brandy snifters, far from the bar, will be feigning conversation and watching how the gray-haired albino will bend down to order the valets tending to the prostrate body on the floor to return to their service posts; our eyes won't be able to fully focus on the ball, because once again, as always, we'll be searching for your face, even though we know that it'll be impossible for us to see it without losing, without losing on the field, so we'll turn our eyes toward a group of haggard nurses entering through the stadium gates. When we send a looping ball into the middle of the canarinho area, we'll slip and fall going up for the header with Honorino; we'll go down and down without the motherfucking *conchesumadre* referee, Yamasaki Maldonado, whistling any foul, a good no-call in the end because in trying to get the header, we'll also have knocked Zózimo down and the bouncing ball will be swept up by Mauro Ramos and sent clear of the area, out across the lateral touchline. The haggard nurses will shoulder their equipment before climbing the stairs, listen: with the guerrillero, we'll throw the ball in to Eladio, with whom, under pressure from Garrincha, always Garrincha, we'll fight to get it to Jorge Toro, but Didí will get a foot in and chip it up to his teammate on the attacking line, making a break, Garrincha will show us with the speed of their combination how, with our backs turned, in some future moment, we'll be able to go down and reverse the ball, how it'll be possible to go to the ground without falling in order to send a pass to the right of their attack, to that place that'll be established as our left side, searching for Vavá. Vavá's position would've been the pivot point for that counterattack if we hadn't been waiting there with Raúl Sánchez, with whom we'll take the ball and send it back to start over from the beginning with our number one, Escuti, thus, several bounces later, we'll boot it toward the right touchline and, again, we won't be able to interrupt this narration for a shadow of you that we want to believe we've just glimpsed in the luxury box, and, again, we won't be able to interrupt ourselves because the haggard nurses are climbing up the stairs toward the prostrate body on the floor there above, and, again, we won't be able to interrupt ourselves down on the pitch where we'll be holding firm with Jorge Toro, both feet finding a spot of surprising green amid these withered grasses; from there, we'll begin to thread together an attacking arrow that, to us, will appear to be ours and plural, for its red glow, and, again, we won't be able to interrupt the flow until the omnipresent forward, Amarildo, comes up from behind and delivers a kick to the sole of our foot. We'll fall and fall and fall *por la* cocksucking *concha*, fucking *mierda*, flogging the air with these taught arms because we won't have a projectile to throw down at the fucking *desgraciado*, nothing of our own to throw at the head of our enemy, yes: but this time the *saquero* referee, Yamasaki Maldonado, blunderer's blunder, will book the infraction, transforming our jeers into cheers as their center forward comes and offers us his hand in apology. We'll set up the free kick with Raúl Sánchez on the left side of that center circle that won't be ours either; for we understood long ago that this field also belongs to the council of directors, reclining in monochrome suits, gagging, grotesquely laughing, or gargling brandy, we won't know, all we'll know now is that we own nothing and nothing owns us: not even one lousy object to throw at the referee, brother of our brother, the next time he makes a call against the eighty thousand, the eight thousand, the eight hundred, the eighty, the eight of us still enduring this cold, brisker now at this sundown hour in June; because the bleachers in these stands still belong to the plush leather seats of the luxury box, we'll end up believing that our defenders will be the base of a new attacking triangle, and yet, the full shape won't yet appear before us. So we'll step up to send the free kick hard across the whole pitch with such fury that the ball will be lost at the intersection of the endline and the outside edge of that area that will no longer seem remote, enticing, resistant. For that reason, our focus will shift away from the group of haggard nurses climbing the stairs to the luxury box, not catching one detail of the medical equipment they're dragging behind them. We'll just narrate how their keeper, Gilmar, will send a searching ball for Zito, who will trap it and send it to Amarildo; they'll close in on that vaguely red box where we'll be retreating with Eyzaguirre, and we'll deflect the ball toward our own endline: getting just enough of a touch on it that referee, Yamasaki Maldonado, will call a corner kick against us, but whatever, Zagallo will set up the ball beside the corner flag, waiting for a rush of canarinho players to come across the withered grasses; just enough that now they'll form a shape we've never seen, an apse, step by step the haggard nurses climb, from one point to another through the area that's nobody's, neither theirs nor ours. And just enough so that now the Brazilian center forwards will outwit us in their formation, just enough so that Zagallo could choose any of them, and just enough so that following a low, short, and soft corner, Garrincha will slash in from our right—not our left—without urgency, overconfident enough so that with our vaguely red defenders we'll be able to do just enough to send it back out across the touchline, just enough—the nurses won't stop upon entering the luxury box, amid the scandalized laughter of the council members—so that you reappear, just a glimpse, your figure behind some workers, paler even than the valets, and just enough so that amid the first aid kits, oxygen machine, and stretchers, you become briefly visible through the cracks in that wall of monochrome suits, gray, black, grieving now because they'll never have come undone over the loss of a colleague before; just enough so that behind them, a turning back reveals the hem of your colorful coat and the tip of your tall leather boot, emerging from behind the bar, just enough; you'll be slipping something into one pocket, not a glove or a piece of paper, not the lighter or the cigarette case either, but an object emptied after performing its definitive act, and just enough: Garrincha will leap into the air, heading Zagallo's corner kick inside the right post of the frame that they say is ours now for a goal, goal, another canarinho goal, just enough. Garrincha will have thrown himself into the open arms of his teammates, surrounding him, and even a smattering of timid applause will replace our expended insults. And yet, a faint gleam, reflecting the last light of the setting sun, just dropping behind the cordillera that has framed the Campos de Sports, will follow you: the flash of that emptied object that might have been a little bottle of poison, a test tube, a tiny unlabeled flask clutched in your glove before you shove your hand deep into your pocket.

Immediately thereafter, in the center circle we'll act as if we're restarting the game with Eladio and Jorge Toro, believing that, with your reappearance, our strategies will be reorganized, now that the canarinho team's second goal will have increased their already enormous advantage. With Jorge Toro, we'll attempt to send the ball back to Eyzaguirre, with whom we'll act as if the ball is getting away from us, succumbing to the pursuit of Zito and Zagallo, appearing to hustle after us until, observing them carefully, we'll realize that they're pretending too, all of us are, near and far, even the ones who lose in the final, in other finals, and in the finals that'll someday be final; each step with the ball, nothing but mimicry, so you'll have another reason to lean on the bar beside the gray-haired albino and smoke, exhaling until the smoke envelops that angular jaw that he'll use to deliver accented instructions to the haggard nurses who, like a *parvá*—a flock of birds—have alighted around the inert body so that, when they rise, nothing will be left on the floor but scraps of food, dropped silverware, and pieces of broken glass. The same thing all over again: under pressure from Zito and Zagallo, we'll try to make them believe that we're going to pass the ball to our wing, Ramírez Banda, perceiving with him that Eyzaguirre is open down the right touchline, and it'll seem that we're going send it back to him, that the right collective shape will have emerged at last, just when we ceased to believe in it: never again a letter, but a horseshoe; a horseshoe discarded on the field that we can pretend to bend down and pick up before making use of it; an attacking horseshoe. With that new found hope, we'll receive the ball back with Eyzaguirre, combining with Ramírez Banda, parallel, in the middle; you'll want to give the impression that you're smoking, that you're leaning on the bar as you bring the filter to your lips, without revealing your face to anyone, then the smoke you're exhaling will envelope the jaw of the gray-haired albino who, in his harsh language, will be playing director of the directors. The game will have consisted of them believing that we're going to enter that area we'll pretend to call theirs, that Zózimo is going to attempt to cut us off and clear the ball; it'll be as if we trapped his clearance with the feet of Jorge Toro, as if, with him, we saw the horseshoe turn into an arrow whose reddish point would be our wing, Ramírez Banda, on the right, and as if we sent him a driven pass along the ground, down that touchline into a space where he would be preparing to fire the ball on goal, and as if we failed to execute our simulated effort with precision: suddenly your smoke would make the gray-haired albino cough, it would appear to us that our attempted shot was too hard and off target, the director of directors would double over, clutching his chest; the haggard nurses would have to connect him to an oxygen tube and, given the speed of the gray-haired albino's affectation, they would drop the stretcher with what was left of the body that'd been lying on the luxury box floor. You would slowly lower one hand to drop the butt of your cigarette and feign fright at the scene by putting the back of your other hand to your forehead, and we, this vacillating murmuration, would loudly mimic disappointment because the ball sailed wide, past that goal that but for our breath would have become a mere simulacrum of antagonism. Then their stealthy keeper, Gilmar, would send it hard toward the part of the pitch that we would call our right. From your coat pocket, your other hand, gloved now, would pull out a diaphanous kerchief to offer to the gray-haired albino, who, for the first time would speak to you directly in his foreign language to express gratitude for the gesture. The goal kick that dropped in the field's center circle would be controlled by Amarildo, who would send it back to Didí so that the mirage could begin to take shape in an inverted arch in the direction of his teammates who, due to the fragility of these forms, we would consider our opponents; because all of them would be now; our view of you in the luxury box would be blocked by two valets who appear to insult and mock the workers who just finished sweeping up the bloody remains left behind by the nurses, already vanishing down the stairs, and we would just glimpse your leather-gloved hand gesturing with a cigarette in the air; maybe you would be discussing something with the gray-haired albino, making some proposal, or translating this narration for him: when Didí passed it to Zito, when Zito gave dimension to the arch shape by sending a long ball to our right to the feet of his outside wing-back, Djalma Santos, who along that side of the pitch would touch a quick pass to Garrincha, and when he, facing off against Jorge Toro and the guerrillero Rodríguez, passed the ball to Vavá to continue his run, maybe a permanent shape would also be drawn on the other side of the pitch that, nevertheless, we wouldn't see, that would disappear because of our interception with Jorge Toro, because of our heel flick to the guerrillero Rodríguez; from the guerrillero to the center we would begin to imitate the base of that formation, and upon imitating it, we would make an unprecedented error: if one thing mattered to us, it was to form another kind of arrow, supported by our vertical run with Eladio, with our arrival to the middle of the pitch, combining with Honorino, getting the ball back from our forward, overlapping with him to the left, and threading a pass in his direction with our midfielder. Such that, with Honorino we would have to move quickly to take control of that area that we might yet turn red, so quickly that we would forget our imitation: they're going to forget their imitation, that would be the last thing we suspect you would've said to the gray-haired albino; that, as long as we're moved by these bodies out on the field, we won't stop, you lie, that if we fight to gain control of an area that's not ours with Honorino and, if before stepping up in front of their goal, the passing lane closed off by Didí and Mauro Ramos, we send the ball to our center forward, Tobar, the diagram of a machine formed of eighty thousand people will set the physical action into motion; and that motion will make the machines of industry run, we'll hear the director of directors answer you in his strange language, then you'll shake your head, laughing or emphatically disagreeing, it's up to us to choose: with our center forward, Tobar, we're going to drop the ball back to set up an attacking strike, but Zózimo will anticipate our choice and get a foot in to block the decisive pass despite the whistle that will bring the action to a momentary halt, because referee Yamasaki Maldonado—

pause for one of the *desgraciado*'s better calls—is going to book Mauro Ramos for his tackle on Honorino. The movement will set your words into motion and your words will set the movement into motion, the gray-haired albino will reply, then pause and wait for your response; our players will be setting up for the free kick, fifteen meters from that box that we'll need to turn into wind, into dust, into our desert, somewhere we can at least go to play during extra time, and that's what we'll discuss with Eladio, Leonel, and Jorge Toro: observing the convexity of the wall the canarinho team will have built, we'll decide that Jorge Toro's foot will have a direct line over the wall and we'll take the shot, not running, just a couple steps up to the soft ball, sending it powerfully goalward, *conchetumadre*, some of us will still have something ready in our mouths to shout in celebration as the ball bends slightly in its trajectory, sailing just wide, past the left post and the beaten keeper, Gilmar, and we'll take off our hats once again to sit back down, spitting out whatever we had left to say. You still won't answer the gray-haired albino. You'll take the time to remove the extinguished cigarette from your mouth, setting it carefully in the ashtray on the bar, hearing our shrieks and lighting another through our cheers and missteps. You'll carefully exhale your first drag, remove one glove, lift your bare hand up, there, to that spot behind your ear that now we'll catch a glimpse of, the place where you'll have begun to twirl various strands of hair around your fingers, glancing up at the dark sky, heavy with neither clouds nor sun, neither moon nor stars, neither day nor night in this Ñuñoa twilight of ours, and without losing composure, the gray-haired albino will turn toward you in an expected gesture: nobody is allowed to make him, someone who has everything, wait for an answer. From the distant keeper, Gilmar, the goal kick will cross the pitch and be tracked down by Amarildo in the center circle, but we'll come running in with Pluto

Contreras to head it away from him; even without aim, we'll have to keep moving, that's the only way to avoid the realization that all of this has been an imitation of something we don't remember, that running all together in a stadium is also the work of others, eighty thousand, eight million setting the machine of victory in motion: we would rather spend every morning and every afternoon pursuing an animal, chased by the police, arriving in the nick of time to rouse a defenseless person from bed, because the earthquake will be beginning again. You'll keep smoking, motionless, listening to our new narration, along with our already watching eyes, you'll have to hold the gaze of the director of directors, almost violent, because you still won't have answered him; your delay will be aided by the telephone in the luxury box beginning to ring again, by the valet hurrying to bring it over, lifting the receiver, and leaving it there for you on the lacquered surface of the bar. Your delay will be aided by hearing how the collective movement will for once be clearly delineated for us by the canarinho players, one of whose anchors will be their midfielder, Zito, to our right, and the ball will go to him after our header with Pluto Contreras that lacked aim because we couldn't stop moving, red, scattered across the pitch, along the edge of this collective shape, a driven pass skimming across the ground to their waiting forward, Vavá, who will trap it along the touchline and begin his run, supported by their wing, Zagallo, moving into our danger area with the ball at his feet, but we'll slide in with Eyzaguirre and, with one foot, send it rolling in the opposite direction, to our right, where we'll track it down with our wing, Ramírez Banda, going on offense; our run will be reflected in the gray-haired albino's expression of offense at your silence, you'll have put one glove back on and will keep smoking, twirling your hair instead of answering his question or the phone call; our offense and his offense will constitute yet another movement that won't stop; and one you won't respond to either, and yet, because you'll have wanted the director of directors to, in his fury, tune his ear to our cheers, our shouts, *vamos, compañeros*, let's do it. We'll interrupt the run we're making with our wing, Ramírez Banda, when confronted with Zito, opting to send a left-footed pass to Jorge Toro and with him, given his broader view, when the afternoon will have already gone, the night won't yet have arrived, and daybreak will still be a long way off, we'll see that our horseshoe has been set into motion, the horseshoe that we'll have picked up out on the field, the horseshoe that once upon a time we'll have found in a ditch, after falling down and getting hurt, drunk, corralled, lacking a larger, calmer, stronger animal than ourselves, and with the rusted iron in our hands we'll have been lifted up by the idea that, just by moving, we might deliver justice with our hands and feet; so, using the horseshoe as design, we'll send the ball with Jorge Toro up to our wing, Ramírez Banda, already crossing midfield, and we'll receive the ball there; but no, we'll shout while running, seeing the gray-haired albino reach out his arm, his hand, his manicured fingernails, and you gracefully bringing your cigarette to your mouth such that his movement appears clumsy because he grabs at thin air, but no: the gray-haired albino, director of another empire, will extend his manicured fingernails to the telephone receiver and take hold of it. No longer is it the time of the horseshoe, but the time of the irruption, we'll realize with our wing, Ramírez Banda, so the mass of our bodies must shift into the shape of the arrow; without hesitation, we'll send the ball to the arrowhead that we'll have glimpsed, streaking red across the yellow-flecked field; the speed of Honorino, whose run will make it look like we're going to rupture something, until, suddenly, we'll go down again, *saquero* ref!, taken down in the semicircle at the top of the opposing area by the feet of their defender, Zózimo, and motherfucking *hueá de mierda*, no whistle to punish the tackle. Zózimo will clear the ball, sending it hard toward our backline, without aim or design, just a succession of bounces on our side of the pitch that will end at the feet of Pluto Contreras, and from here onward we won't be able to stop, no; the manicured nails of the gray-haired albino won't have touched you, his gaze won't catch your eye: he'll just watch you smoke in silence, listening to us, pulling the phone cord across the lacquered surface of the bar. From here onward, with Pluto Contreras, we won't stop moving, though we'll move through different collective shapes, a W, an H, a horseshoe, the inverted ogival formation no longer facing the sky but directed at our bodies; we'll trap the ball with the feet of Eyzaguirre, the logic of the arrow will only serve us for one attack, a forceful strategy that we'll plot with the feet of Eladio, over to Pluto Contreras, then dropping it back to Raúl Sánchez, and, with him, swinging it around to our keeper, Escuti, where we'll multiply our movements: bouncing the ball, coalescing into position, a murmuration; we'll send a careful ball out to Jorge Toro, controlling it with the skill in his knees, waist, and foot with which we'll follow through too high, such that the force of our pass to our wing, Ramírez Banda, breaking down the right sideline, will be excessive, and excessive our rage, our arrow, our desire to push up and attack. Excessive we eighty thousand, we eight million excessively forceful people will be, and for that reason we can't let them stop us; we'll hurry with shouts, insults, and spittle for our comrades on the other team as they take their throw. Nilton Santos will throw the ball to Didí and, as the gray-haired albino drags the telephone receiver across the bar in front of you, you'll give a slight flick with a gloved finger to the butt of your cigarette and all its ash will fall on his manicure: that hand will burn and, though scorching, we'll see that the directors of directors won't scream, won't jump, won't even defend himself against a physical attack: the directors' thing will always be to sit back in their plush leather seats, to drink from glasses of varying size, to laugh at the weak, and to fall asleep while making sure that their workers never stop moving; Didí will pass it to Zagallo, from the angle of his torso his teammates will apprehend where to position themselves in the attacking wave, at a jog, Zagallo will swerve toward the center of the pitch, he'll turn away from the pressure we'll bring with Jorge Toro and our wing, Ramírez Banda, and he won't have any option but to send it ahead to Amarildo, who will tremble just intuiting the integrity of the shape they know so well, quickly sending a cross the width of the pitch to Garrincha, always on our left. We'll cheer and throw our arms into the air, taking advantage of the moment to glance up at the luxury box and see how the gray-haired albino answers the phone call with his burned hand and, stammering, repeats his greeting, because he can't believe that the person on the other end of the line has hung up on him: absorbed in yelling at the operator, he'll miss the mirthful oscillation of your head, laughing; after taking a few steps with the ball, Garrincha will gesture too, he'll be studying our movements with the guerrillero Rodríguez; we'll sweep at his feet and he'll whisk the ball away, eluding us and looking ahead to the frontline of that wave he's building with Vavá and Amarildo. They'll be waiting for him so they can push up together toward the goal that we'll have turned red, and so absorbed in staring at it, Garrincha won't notice the red shirt of the player coming at him, the red shirt of our guerrillero Rodríguez, and just as he turns to escape us, we'll step up with Raúl Sánchez too; so his elusive move won't be enough to outmaneuver our number and we'll strip the ball away from him and take off running with it, delivering it to Jorge Toro in the middle, the nock of our sharpened arrow beginning with him, and with him we'll run with the ball, drawing a vertical line through the center circle of the pitch. At the bar, the gray-haired albino will have gotten the operator to place an international call for him, giving him the opportunity to scream in his foreign language, unintelligible insults that he'll direct at you with his eyes, because he'll believe you to be absorbed in our narration as it comes through the loudspeaker in the stands: to the left, we'll begin drawing the second diagonal of the arrow with Leonel and, thrilled to receive the ball from Jorge Toro, instead of pushing up in the same direction, we'll choose to add a horizontal line to the arrowhead with a long pass to our right antipode on the pitch, our wing, Ramírez Banda, scrawling with him the left diagonal line, but no, repeating the parallel line back to Leonel, because we can't stop if we want to catch a glimpse of your face up in the luxury box, to see if you're laughing with your glove in your mouth or just distractedly touching your teeth when the gray-haired albino holds the receiver up to your face, emphasizing his guttural shrieks: *goal-oriented, goal-oriented*, will be what his booming voice repeats, reddened face, shoulders back on the bar about to throw the phone receiver over the railing of the luxury box, but instead, he'll just hang up, order two glasses of sparkling water that the barman will immediately present on a tray, and, as soon as they're in front of him, the director of directors will drink them down, bringing a cloth napkin to his mouth, patting dry the sweat on his forehead, and then giving you a grin, despite the fact that you'll be too busy turning your back on us to respond to him, listening to how, then, we'll send an identical pass back to the other side with Leonel, receiving it for the umpteenth time with our wing, Ramírez Banda, on the right; but if the arrow doesn't pierce the target, it'll disintegrate in the air, and that too will be movement, so Zito will interrupt the broken shape, stopping our attack and blithely sending a driven ball bouncing and rolling and slowing back to the feet of their stout keeper, Gilmar.

Up in the luxury box, the barman will have set two more glasses of sparkling water in front of the gray-haired albino, while your fellow council members will be stretching and adjusting themselves in their armchairs, their mouths only opening to utter insipid opinions about the business deals they're always getting offered, sitting down to fancy dinners, outside their sports' clubs, and in the bathrooms of exclusive brothels; a steal, people say; a dime a dozen, a knickknack, a sad joke, they'll respond in their suits of blue, gray, beige, black, and at the bar you'll remove a pearlescent watch from your coat pocket, staring at it and listening to us on the radio: the opposing keeper, Gilmar, will send the goal kick downfield, all the way to Didí and Amarildo, who will attempt to possess the ball, unsuccessfully, because we'll intercept it with Raúl Sanchez and send it back into the area we're trying to advance into, attacking, cutting through their defenses. And the ball will drop toward Leonel, our left wing, with whom, at midfield, we'll head it toward Jorge Toro, and with him we'll send a through-ball to a streaking Eladio. The gray-haired albino will interrupt your listening, persistently urging you to accept the glass of sparkling water, and when you do, his eyes will latch for a second onto your pearlescent watch. Then he'll turn away; with a stiff arm and raised index finger, he'll give an order to one of the valets and then lean unexpectedly close to your ear and, in the lowest of voices, nostrils flared and eyes extremely wide, he'll whisper something, something that'll make you stand up from your seat at the bar, take a step back, and give a vague response, never turning to face us, in a language neither ours nor that of your fellow council members: but there will be no need for translation, you'll tell him no, no, no, and then you'll move across the luxury box, smoking, as if some imminence depended on you no longer listening, knowing full well that we'll send a parallel cross to the left with Eladio, that we'll combine once again with Leonel to keep the movement of our collective arrow in the air, collective in the way we spread out across the field. We'll pause with Leonel, possessing the ball and reading the developing rush, under pressure from Djalma Santos, who, like everyone else, will be awaiting our next move. But instead of sending the ball on and sticking to how the play diagramed, we'll attempt to release our pent-up rage by taking the defenders on one by one, dribbling the ball, listen: him or us. And it won't work, apparently, because Djalma Santos will strip the ball away with his instep and send it out of bounds across the left touchline of our attacking end; up in the luxury box, from the mouth of the gray-haired albino, words will ring out at high volume, words that, for a moment, will be superimposed over our narration on the radio, words incomprehensible to us, to the valets, to the barmen, to the nurses, and to the assistants, and though we won't understand them at first, your fellow council members—sitting in their plush leather seats, at the buffet table, at the bar—will rise to their feet as one; here, one clears his throat, there, another pulls a comb out of his pocket to fix his hair, a third adjusts his tie, and in the back another will freshen up, dabbing the skin on his face with cologne, while you, with your back turned, still smoking, will pause your movement, recovering the expectant calm needed to carry out the next phase of your plan: we'll take the throw with the guerrillero Rodríguez, sending it to Eladio in the middle, touching it with him on to Jorge Toro, the pass tracing the vertical line of the arrow's center; the ball's trajectory will be deflected by Didí but will bounce back to Honorino, and we'll make a run with him before delivering the ball to Jorge Toro on the inside, touching it right back to Honorino, and in the vertiginous rush we won't care about Zito's handball, that referee Yamasaki Maldonado, little piece of shit, *hermanito de mierda*, ignores the violation, because we'll have received another one-touch pass from Honorino back to Jorge Toro, with whom we'll maintain possession, advancing steadily with an open view of the goal our arrow is aiming at, keeping the ball on our left foot as we streak ahead, outstripping the pursuit of Didí and Zito. Our run will look strong and dynamic, the athletic moves of a crack player, but then, from the perspective of Jorge Toro, we'll see the collective arrow shape shifting into position and we'll know that Leonel—with whom, off the ball, we've made an unmarked run, deep into the canarinho area, our attacking end—will have gotten open on the far left side, so the through-ball we'll send with Jorge Toro, parallel to the touchline, will easily reach its target; what we'll soon realize is that, up in the luxury box, several valets will now be intensely engaged in the work of bringing out multiple boxes from behind the bar, and out of those boxes they'll begin unpacking golden bottles of champagne on silver trays; seeing Mauro Ramos standing guard at the near post, with Leonel we'll consider passing the ball to Honorino in the middle, at the point of the arrow, but no: our flow will remain pure movement, not seeing the best way to direct it toward that space of mesh, net, threads, wires, and cables, so we'll opt for the direct shot at the opponent's goal, an individual and futile attempt, because our effort with Leonel will have blurred our vision, making us lose sight of the plural shape, just a cluster of directors there above watching us, on their feet and you behind them, your back turned, as we fall to the grass exhausted.

As Gilmar's goal kick sails across sky of the dark winter afternoon at the Campos de Sports, we'll see how, up in the luxury box, the valets are hurrying to wash, dry, and line up champagne flutes on the bar. Through their crystal, we'll see how you've slipped away into a shadowy corner where only your coat will be visible against the darkness, below the speakers, where you will listen to us, and we'll wish we could hear you: this time Amarildo won't trap the ball as it drops, because we'll direct it with Pluto Contreras's head back to Eyzaguirre, slightly behind and to our right, and from there we'll send it low and hard to our wing, Ramírez Banda, with whom we'll skirt the right touchline, chased by Zagallo, by the eyes of your fellow council members up in the luxury box, by the wild screams of enthusiasm that we'll release, rushing onward, and just as it'll seem we're on the verge of collectively remembering the one thing that'll bring it all together, it'll slip away into oblivion; they'll try to take the ball, but we'll be convinced that there are more of us than of them, more cheers and whistles for us, so when Zagallo takes the ball and passes it back to Nilton Santos it'll bounce off our wing, Ramírez Banda, and out across the touchline. The opposing defender will take the throw, dropping it at the feet of Zito, who will send it back to the defender, who, from there, under pressure from our wing, Ramírez Banda, and our center forward, Tobar, will find Mauro Ramos in the middle; Ramos will make a run, leaving first one and then another of our red shirts behind and then sending a pass to his left to Nilton Santos as, there above, the champagne flutes are still being lined up on the bar, sparkling, sanitized with scalding steam, an unfamiliar sight in our Chilean winters; they'll dry the flutes with cloths thicker and finer than our garments, patched up once again last summer, convinced that, yes, at this World Cup semifinal, yes: and yes what?, we'll end up asking ourselves, because we'll no longer recall any of that, out here in the cold, at this twilight hour, neither day nor night now. And we won't feel any urgency to answer that question beyond the urgency of our center forward, Tobar, with whom we'll rush at the opposing wingback, causing Nilton Santos to send the ball, hard, past us, to Amarildo on the right. With the canarinho attack wave not yet fully formed, the opposing striker will flip the ball ahead into space, passing it to himself, tracking it down and leaving us, with Eladio, behind; Amarildo's run will pick up speed and he'll swing it over to Vavá, off to his side and in the direction of the area that might still be ours, because we'll protect it with a sliding tackle from Eladio, both feet out, as thoughtless as it is dangerous but successful in taking the ball back: the referee, Yamasaki Maldonado, will have brought his whistle to his lips, but won't blow it, o executioner mine executioner, and no call, no foul, just a flashing gleam, no longer red but yellow, in our eyes, from the lights that, at that hour, will have come on above the Estadio Nacional at the Campos de Sports. Under the lights, with Eladio, we'll make a second effort and quickly drive the ball along the ground, across midfield, to Jorge Toro, with whom we'll send it down our right touchline, deep into the Brazilian half in the direction of our wing, Ramírez Banda, and with all that electricity flowing, we'll be spurred on, thinking that the lights will help our vision, that maybe now we'll be able to glimpse your face, even if you're still hidden up in the luxury box, there in the only remaining vein of shadow in the bright stadium, aware that off to one side the valets will have begun to pour champagne into the fluted glasses; we'll convince ourselves that the lights are illuminating our effort, running at both ends of the pitch to invert the horseshoe shape that we'll naturally have fallen into, and Nilton Santos will cut off the run we're making with our wing, Ramírez Banda, by striking the ball and sending it sailing back toward midfield and we'll move to track it down with our center forward, Tobar, at the same time as Zózimo, who with a shoulder will move us out of the way and trap it and then send it over to Vavá on our right, near midfield, and for a second we'll remember that we're the ones who will have to pay for all of that electricity that the stadium lights of the owners are casting down on our faces and, with Eyzaguirre, we'll throw the whole of our enraged body at them; their player's advance will be stopped, though the ball will continue on, sailing out into touch. While going to take the throw with Eyzaguirre, we'll realize now, with Honorino, that the stadium lights weren't installed to give us greater clarity; and we'll also forget, as we race forward, tireless, exhausted, dripping with sweat, that it'll take equal effort to tear them down, and with Honorino we'll hug that touchline, because we've never been comfortable out to the right, and so, at full speed, we'll trace a diagonal line toward the point of our collective arrow shape and, with skillful dribbling, we'll leave Didí, Zózimo, and another canarinho player behind and, right at their backline, the ball will get away from us, right before reaching our center forward, Tobar, at the point of that arrow, and in that exact moment, because of the effect of the stadium lights, high overhead on their towers, we'll clearly see our shadows outlined on the grass, stretched longer than the fluted glasses of your fellow council members up in the luxury box; now the rows of pristine crystal flutes will be filled with champagne, golden, their glow preventing us from finding your face: all we'll see are the gray-haired albino's hands folded across his chrome-colored suit, in the center of the luxury box and, around him, your fellow council members, with an expectant air, grimaces at the ready because the loose ball will drop to our left, at the feet of Djalma Santos, who will escape our pressure with Leonel and strike the ball hard, hurrying, with no regard for the position of his teammates in their attacking wave that'll break right there and be swept back in an undertow. That shift in our favor will make it easy to intercept the ball with the guerillero Rodríguez, and from there send it on to Jorge Toro, at the nock of the arrow to keep us from devolving into a new horseshoe shape, and then, facing pressure on all sides from Didí and Garrincha, we'll pass it directly to Eladio at the field's central axis. With Eladio we'll have time and space within the shape, or so we'll think; we'll try to possess the ball, to conceal it, waiting for the shape of our attack, an arrow or a horseshoe, to be defined by the rest of our red shirts and not by the gleam of the stadium lights reflecting off the crystalline line of two dozen champagne flutes; in that way, we'll even lose sight of your shadow, there above, in the luxury box, because only the directors and not the blinded workers will remain fully illuminated. We'll pass it to the right to Eyzaguirre, with whom, looking for the next link, black spots in our eyes, we'll get confused as we try contain the ball just as Zagallo steps up, and yet we'll instinctively turn back toward our line of red defenders on the right; getting support from Raúl Sánchez, with whom we'll send it back to Eyzaguirre, and from his position we'll redefine our attacking shape, not with a forced mutation of one play-design into another, but with a full swing across the horseshoe, such that, out of its very substance, we'll be able to forge an arrow: we'll pass the ball to Pluto Contreras in the center, from him we'll look for Eladio, but the pass will be off target, allowing Didí to cut it off with speed and make a run and deliver a pass to his teammate, Garrincha, who, once again, will have found a way to maneuver into wide-open space, goddamit!, but Didí's pass will be behind him and the ball will hit him in the back and bounce out to our left, where we'll be waiting with the guerillero Rodríguez to break the attacking canarinho wave and to begin, with our wing, Ramírez Banda, to rebuild our arrow as we move back up the pitch. With two runs, we'll already have delineated the apex, and so, with our wing, we'll send the ball from the right side of the pitch ahead to connect with our center forward, Tobar, and with him we'll continue to define our shape, with a high, diagonal pass into the middle, to the point of the arrow now established with Honorino, with whom we'll leap into the air, failing to comprehend how the flying Zózimo gets there first, and his header will clear the ball far from the center circle of that distant area, and the more we'll move the more un-moving your fellow council members will remain, there above in the luxury box, the lights now fully illuminating their suits, well-groomed haircuts, and cufflinks, their briefcases and fountain pens, their safe deposit boxes, contracts, and constitutions, but not you; the ball will escape us, moving right toward Mauro Ramos, we'll stop trying to locate you in order to counter that clearance with a powerful header and a run with our center forward, Tobar, seeking to possess the ball; and yet, it'll be one of the opposing strikers, Vavá, who will track it down and send it out across the right touchline. The lights will make us glance up, searching for you, and though we'll no longer even glimpse the shadow of your coat, we'll intuit that, for you, there will be no reason for us to await an explosion of laughter and electricity and uncorking of bottles: we'll have forgotten about all of that anyway, hurrying, quickly, with the hands of Eyzaguirre, to make the throw down the touchline to Honorino, with whom we'll run with the ball all the way to the little flag in the corner, taunting Nilton Santos with the ball, showing it to him and taking it away, until he'll lose patience and with a sliding tackle knock us, *La Roja*, to the ground: you must hear the whistle blow, justice and plunder, of the referee, Yamasaki Maldonado, calling a free kick on the right side of our attacking end, just outside the canarinho area. We'll notice a little quiver in one corner of the luxury box, that spot where none of your fellow council members will be standing, exaggeratedly smil-ing: the movement of your head there, sheltered in your coat and smoking, whose angle will lead us to guess that your eyes will be fixed on the effervescence of those fluted glasses, and now, with that, we'll boil over; our gaze, an arrow, an oblique arrow, from here, seeking the goal whose impregnability we'll have forgotten. From now on, our scorn will be total, stunned because the defense of the world champions will have clustered together, occupying that entire area, and so, with Jorge Toro, we won't take a direct shot, rather we'll send a pass into the middle, where we'll be rushing forward at full speed with Eyzaguirre from the edge of the area, convinced that now the point of the arrow will come into the light, bubbling and foaming and golden, not the red of our shirts on the pitch, and so we'll send a pass toward the penalty marker and yet that pass will be blocked by Mauro Ramos. And when the ball comes back to us at the feet of Eyzaguirre, now at the vertex formed by the goal line and the right touchline, Mauro Ramos will be there to strip the ball away from us and attempt to clear it, sweeping it up onto the counterattacking wave that they'll fail to catch, because, once again, the wave will break into an undertow, because in making their run, they'll have forgotten something too; we'll easily overtake them, running with our wing, Ramírez Banda, we'll strip the ball away from them and manage, in our distraction, still trying to catch sight of your face, to send another searching pass into the center of the canarinho area, and once again our effort will be cut off by the header of another, of Zózimo, clearing the ball out to Didí, who in turn will flick it on with his head. With Eyzaguirre, we'll hold firm at that spot, part of the rusted old horseshoe, the shape with which we'll have learned to defend, and we'll switch the direction of the ball, passing it over to our wing, Ramírez Banda, and sending it right back with him, because by now we'll also have learned that, in order to attack, we must use the shape of the red arrow, with a copper arrowhead; after all this effort, we'll have only two goals we can use and accept as our own, and upon receiving the ball with our wing, Ramírez Banda, we'll proceed to trace a diagonal line that, we'll be aware with Eyzaguirre, we need to connect, through the center, to another horizontal line: a pass to Pluto Contreras, with whom we'll make the ball circulate back to the base, tracing the vertical line along which we'll run, moving up with Eladio; and, with him, we'll pierce the semicircle at the top of the canarinho area, establishing the final link, just as a tackle from Zito, motherfucking *conchesumadre*, will knock us off balance and, with a movement of the purest kind, send us falling to the ground. Now, you'll begin to move out of your corner in the luxury box, preparing for the decisive strike, while your fellow council members are exchanging enthusiastic words in different languages, finally; now, all eyes will be drawn to the gray-haired albino, who will stretch out his platinum arm and signal the head-valet, indicating that he should ready the trays, just as the whistle of the arbiter of injustice, Yamasaki Maldonado, will blow, calling the foul, a free kick twelve steps outside the Brazilian area, and we'll scream at the opposing team, telling them to go fuck themselves, *que se vayan a la chucha*, gripped by rage at the fact that Zito's blatant foul won't be punished with a booking: and we want your fellow council members to move, move, to let us see you through that crowd who, laughing, will hover around the gray-haired albino at the railing of the luxury box, expectant, while behind them we'll finally catch sight of you making a move that we would never have noticed if not for the pause in the action, as we await the free kick: from your pocket, once again you'll take out the little bottle, the test tube, the flask, and suddenly we'll see how, in front of the trays, you open it over the foaming bubbles, above the fluted glasses, glowing and unguarded in that moment because all the valets will have assembled around the gray-haired albino to receive their latest instructions, and then your figure, turning, will disappear back into the far corner; you'll take cover behind the hovering directors and listen, from the speakers, to how the canarinho team will have finally formed a wall at the semicircle at the top of their area; and how we'll be distracting them there, in the middle, with our center forwards, surrounding them with our wings, moving at angles that will replicate those of the chalk lines, waiting for a pass, for the chance to redirect the ball or, in all that enthusiasm, for you to reveal your face. We'll set up in front of the ball with Jorge Toro, take a step back, hope not to forget ourselves and, instead, find a way to only see what's right in front of us, to understand that the plural movement so long aspired to will, now, stop us, and that, from this moment on, we'll no longer be we in the future tense, because the collective pause ends when we allow ourselves to be interrupted and ruptured, when we let you make the decisions: so be it, let us lose ourselves to keep from losing: Jorge Toro runs, bends forward, strikes the ball, it goes up, over the wall, subtly bending to the left in its trajectory and, in that parabola, enters the upper corner of the goal, and it's a goal, goal, goal, goal, goal for the Chilean team! The crowd is going wild, gentlemen: arms aloft, handkerchiefs seat cushions and signs flapping, and everywhere red—or, better, tricolor—flags waving, while the Chilean players embrace Jorge Toro and up in the luxury box, all the heads of the international conglomerates in attendance at this magnificent World Cup of Soccer, pride of the Chilean people, congratulate our directors for having tightened the score with a simple champagne toast, to the health of the competitive spirit, reaching its true climax with this achievement. Though there are only three short minutes left before the end of the first half of this match, the hopes of the players and of the eight, eight thousand, eight million, I mean, eighty thousand spectators at this unforgettable semifinal have been renewed, gentlemen: with two goals, Brazil is still ahead, and yet Chile has added one and is only one goal away from tying the game, with victory maybe even in sight, and you'll already have vanished down the stairs, the person on the other end of the phone line will have understood that now, indeed, it is only you and her, no one else, and we'll never get a chance to see you, your look of satisfaction, our faces aglow with happiness at the renewed possibility of reaching the final and hoisting the cup: I dare say, dear listeners, that we should expect the best for the future of this game, even if our national and international directors up in the luxury box appear to have fallen into a state of friendly discord, returning to their seats where lifelessly they sit. I must apologize now, because we're being told that it's no laughing matter and that some of them have dropped to the floor; nevertheless, the authorities immediately call for calm, a team of doctors and nurses is already on the scene to attend to the severe mass intoxication that unfortunately has stricken the entire directorial cohort of this majestic event. We'll bring you more information shortly about this developing situation that, no doubt, is perfectly under control. In the meantime, let's return to the pitch, where the Brazilian team is getting back into action. Vavá sends it back to Djalma Santos, who stretches it over to Mauro Ramos. In the final minutes of this first half, our hopes for victory, yes sir, remain untarnished, as long as we have our crack players out there representing us on the pitch: after the brilliant goal by Jorge Toro, we can be sure that, for Chile, anything is possible, because with the feet of our team, we'll make history as one people, one nation, and one country of winners.

3

PERSPECTIVE OF THE FLOCK

THE COMMENTATOR BOARDS the train car, settles into one of the opposing seats after helping an elderly couple put their small suitcase into the overhead compartment; his own trunk is in the luggage car, fitting perfectly among forty-seven other pieces—he was given that number by the boy who was stowing them. Fitting perfectly, he repeats. All he has with him are his glasses, wallet, and pocket watch. Five will be the number of passengers accompanying him in that car from Santiago back to Temuco. Just five for this first leg, he observes. And he takes in their movements calmly, arms and feet, shoulders and knees that like his own flex, bend, lean, begin to sway in unison, vibrating against the leather, each one looking at the same thing outside, fingers of distinct thicknesses rising toward the platform. The shape begins to move, it's being formed, it's about to show him who and in what position when the door between cars opens, a waiter walks in, and the structure shifts again, always: now there are six, but the waiter's stay only lasts for a few fast-moving houses out the window; and yet, the obliging smile is not reciprocated by the movements of the people in the car; he comes in as, for a second, the setting sun peaks between the cypresses, already in a rural area, and disappears behind a long brick wall that finds the same five faces reflected in the windows.

"Welcome aboard the express train, sir. The afternoon newspapers?"

The commentator smiles. He accepts the papers with a movement of his head, he's realized he should let another diagram take shape: in that moment, he sees the same obliging smile, the same flexed neck, the identical napkin folded over the forearm of six waiters and waitresses in each car of the express train.

"Sparkling water? Coffee? Papaya soda, wine, pisco sour, Bilz?"

"A boldo tea, if you would be so kind."

Then the commentator combines the movement of changing his hat's location, from on top of the table to the opposite seat, with the muttering of another passenger behind him, with the sighs of an aunt, a mother, and her daughter in the back—the laughter of the daughter—and with the silent movement with which the old man opens a wood and metal case, out of which he and his wife start taking dominoes one by one—post after post out the window, tree after tree—and setting them up on the surface of a hardcover book on one of their laps; the commentator combines each of those actions with those of his own fingers as they fold the afternoon papers and set them down on one side of his seat, and as he does so, he forces himself to open his eyes, to move, to stay present in the time and place that the Santiago-Temuco express train is passing through, to let that diagram continue to take shape.

And with that decision, all the other diagrams that present themselves to him are left behind. The possible trajectories and combinations as well, he hopes; but if he voices it like this, in these terms, there will also be a possibility of harmony about to reveal itself, because each one of those concepts includes its own realization, such that he should pick up a newspaper, any newspaper, and sit there reading the headline: "Chile Takes Third Place in World Cup" because its ink gives off a powerful odor, the type barely printed on the industrial paper, the blurry photographs, the arrangement previously laid out on a surface, the successive lines, below the shot of Garrincha raising the trophy, the golden ball, in his hands, and, to one side, after a thin line that traverses the middle of the page, a column of text. The commentator has decided to extend the inertia of the bodies around him to the whole trip, without speaking to or about them; he wants to let the dominoes connect, the trunks, suitcases, boxes, and bags to fit in the luggage car, the sounds with which the aunt, the mother, and the daughter don't speak to remain the noise of noses, the headlines of the afternoon papers to be nothing more than stains, rust, *pjñén* of yesterday, words so transparent that they fade away before being seen, and every blade of rolling yellow field out the window reveals a part of the hillside that just passed by, of the hillside, of the foothills, of the mountains, of the cordillera in the distance, his gaze that doesn't see his own reflection in the glass, but looks out at the landscape: he was walking in the foothills hand in hand with his *Fjcha* when he noticed for the first time that the flock, the murmuration, the *parvá* of *xjuxjú* and the embers of the wind were two very different things, that the leaves of *ñjre*, *pegjn*, and *lawal* were swirling, moving toward the river or through the crevice, indifferent to his vision, to the booming voice of his *Fjcha*, to the proximity of his footsteps to the waterfall; it was the foothills, something entirely different than a hillside, the commentator avoids repeating himself, reclining in his seat with the winter sun on his face; he no longer has to care about the rising moisture in the ravines, the height of the *pegjn*, or the impenetrability of the thicket of *foj*, because the foothills just passed by and he is making an effort to keep his eyes trained out window; on the other side of the foothills, the field; it's all field, his *Fjcha* bellows again, and when his neck is released he runs to frighten the flock of *xjuxjú* that are pecking about, not out of malice nor to prepare the earth for when the strong men, the *wæxes*, with their *paljnes* come up from the river, but to watch that blur of canary-yellow, gray, white in the air that oscillates, for a moment concealing the sun that illuminates them, the *xjuxjú* turn back and, as they descend toward him, innumerable, he realizes that they are looking back at him, that they're landing just out of reach of his small hands and his *pjñjñentos* feet: without realizing it, he releases a giggle of fascination into the air, keening laughter that in his throat is chirping, chirping of *xjuxjú* that respond with a warning in the moment that other *wæxes* arrive from beyond the road, sending the *xjuxjú* to wing because the *wæxes* have brought a ball of pig skin that frightens them. He moves away in pursuit of the shadow left by the flock, while his *Fjcha* with a single word makes the *wæxes* play: it's all field, *paljn* or foot, but never hands, because hands are for work, hunting, harvest, and to give him a beating; it's all field, but he remains at the edge of it all, already a narrator, watching how the shadow of the flock directs the strong men in their dance, the yellow shadow that chooses where there will be less heat so that's where they push, hit, get dirty, spit, and celebrate. There are no rules, his *Fjcha* answers when he hears him ask with a chirp and when the *wæxes* also start paying attention to his rasping in the autumn when his voice changes; there are no rules, his *Fjcha* reveals to him, his *Fjcha* and the *Fjcha* of everyone who lives beyond the foothills. But when the *wæxes* arrive from the other side of the big water, his *Fjcha* asks him not to sing the goals or to stand watching the flock. Instead, if the *maxj* come to play, he gargles and reads their books, there are parties, rhythms, kissing, unions; those women celebrate him, make him pretty, and take him to the river to bathe with them, even though his narrations make them lose the final game to the *wæxes* of the mountains, until one night his *Fjcha* finds him with them in the river, under a full moon, transformed and, without speaking to them, as if they never heard him before, he throws them out of the game, forbids them from returning and him from continuing to sing the games. He hides in the caves, learns that the worms, the ants, the bees, and the invisible creatures are also flocks with names, that they also vocalize in his way. When he decides to return, his *Fjcha* is as wrinkled as a stone, the train and the trucks and a factory have come to the foothills, the *xjuxjú* are gone, the ground is bare because now the canopies of the *ñjre*, *pegjn*, and *lawal* are full of *xile*, pitch-black birds with a yellow line across their breasts, the males mispronounced, the females the color of lead, the humidity of the valleys has become sticky, the *pegjn* grows sparse, bearing a salty fruit and swapping the impenetrability of the *foj* for a money tree, just one in the middle of the grove. The penultimate day, the *wæxes* arrive from across the big water with shirts of all the same color, they come following a man in black: he is a judge, they claim; they want that judge to replace his *Fjcha*, but the people of the foothills get angry and expel them from the game too. Nevertheless, the owners of the trains, the trucks, and the factory return and insist, threatening them with fire. The man in black is installed during the summer, he's followed by a large flock of *xile* that only open their beaks to eat and don't easily respond to his narrator's voice; the man in black brings written rules; hands yes, but only as last recourse; no *paljnes*. And only in their foreign names. His *Fjcha* refuses, naturally. The owners demonstrate that they know more of fire, one *wæxé* loses patience and shoots, the flock immediately takes to wing and ascends into the heights. His *Fjcha* is forced to flee and hide out in the depths of the ravine, with the *maxj*; the next day he's found dead, floating in the river. The owners publish newspapers and broadcast television shows telling how the *maxj* assassinated his

Fjcha because he refused to bathe in the river with them. But it's a lie. He knows. So, he rises before dawn, chirps, expectorates, laughs, crunches a nut, whistles, tweets, sings, vociferates, and joins the millions of *xile* that have arrived that summer; makes them rise, makes them flap, and at midday sends them at the factory's biggest chimney, at the train engine; there are two explosions, at last the fire is unleashed with gunshots, fires and burnings throughout the area. Two of the *maxj* are taken prisoner, the owners take charge of viciously applying the law to them, they are sentenced to life, though their daughter is taken to the youth home of the rail workers, called the Ferrobádminton club, in the capital. The *maxj* are erased from the map of history; apart from the director, the narrator revises, no longer seeing a single light in the night that comes in through the window of the train car. The people of the hills are disbanded, they migrate to the cities. But it's a lie. He knows. So he rises before dawn, chirps, expectorates, laughs, crunches a nut, whistles, tweets, sings, vociferates, and like everyone else, he decides to go to the capital, to learn all the names, to enroll in school, to get a journalism degree, to work at the radio for decades, to call one last game before taking the Santiago-Temuco express train that, in the middle of the night, goes off the tracks on a new bridge, built over a ravine in the foothills, because of a technical failure in its construction, is the last thing he says.

CARLOS LABBÉ, one of *Granta*'s "Best Young Spanish-Language Novelists," was born in Chile and is the author of ten novels, including *Navidad & Matanza*, *Loquela*, and *Spiritual Choreographies* (all available from Open Letter), three collections of short stories, and a book of essays. In addition to his writings he is a musician, and has released four albums. He is part of the literary collective Sangría, based in Santiago and Brooklyn.

WILL VANDERHYDEN has translated fiction by Carlos Labbé, Rodrigo Fresán, Fernanda García Lao, Andrés Felipe Solano, and Rodolfo Enrique Fogwill, among others. He has received two translation fellowships from the National Endowment for the Arts (2016 and 2023) and a residency fellowship from the Lannan Foundation (2015). His translation of *The Invented Part* by Rodrigo Fresán won the 2018 Best Translated Book Award.

WILL VANDERHYDEN received an MA in Literary Translation Studies from the University of Rochester. He has translated fiction by Carlos Labbé, Edgardo Cozarinsky, Alfredo Bryce Echenique, Juan Marsé, Rafael Sánchez Ferlosio, Rodrigo Fresán, and Elvio Gandolfo. He received NEA and Lannan fellowships to translate another of Fresán's novels, *The Invented Part.*